MOUNTAIN MAN BOOTS

HUNTS A KILLER ON THE LOOSE

A WESTERN ADVENTURE

GENE TURNEY

ISBN: 9798859148653

This novel, as are all my novels and everything I do, is dedicated to Cheryl, my children, grandchildren, nieces, nephews, cousin Pat, other in-laws and outlaws, and many friends' encouragements. Without the faith and encouragement of so many, this book would not exist. With great appreciation, I acknowledge the people who have provided invaluable assistance to the development of this particular novel.

FOREWORD

Mountain Man Boots McCray is said to have lived a charmed life in the Rocky Mountains. There is no charm to it, he claims. His life comes from knowing he can be the odds of life-changing events. Boots encounters a man from his past that turns out to be a good friend. He encounters a man who shoots holes in a deck of cards, and he helps his wife through her grief when her father dies. Her father is the Chief of the Cheyenne on the mountain, and it looks as though one day, she may become the first woman Cheyenne chief.

1

Mountain man Boots Mc Cray sat on a huge flat rock that connected to a cave that Boots called home. His legs were crossed and he enjoyed his first-morning coffee of the day. Normally, this time of the day and the coffee meant a relaxing time for Boots. However, this morning, he felt a little uneasy in his gut. Over the years, he learned to trust that feeling.

The crisp air contained an aroma Boots knew all too well as Migisi joined him for a morning coffee.

"A mother cat came here last night. She has two cubs, I think."

"Did you see her?"

"I know she was here."

Boots learned to trust Migisi when she told him of

things like this. He continued to look around as he drank his coffee.

"She is gone now. I don't know where she stays, but this was an unusual stop for her."

It was almost as though Migisi had the mountain lion's head on her mind. She continued to tease Boots.

"Cheyenne people know these things. We are one with animals and nature."

Migisi did not tell Boots she saw the mountain lion during one of her trips during the night. She knew he would be upset if she woke him, and he would immediately set about to track down the big cat.

Mountain man Boots Mc Cray knew more than he wanted to know about mountain lions. He had scars on his back to prove it. The big cat did not survive, but, thanks to Migisi's medical skills, Boots is walking today.

"I think we should find her. The two burros and the mustang won't stand a chance in that corral if she decided to come back. I would like to chase her to a new territory. She can take her little ones with her."

Migisi already guessed at Boots' reaction. She dropped two packs on the rock porch beside him. Boots grinned and looked up at Migisi who stood with her fists on her hips.

"Are you going with me, or do you want to sit there all day?"

Boots sprung to his feet and picked up one of the packs while Migisi shouldered the other one.

"I can smell her. I will lead, you follow."

Boots knew better than to argue with his wife. He already checked on the mustang and burros and gave them an extra portion of feed. Boots noted they were still nervous knowing the big cat was in the area.

Migisi stopped walking about two hundred yards from the entrance to the cave. She pointed to a tree limb where the carcass of a deer lay across the limb. A puddle of dry blood showed on the leaves beneath the deer.

"She will come back and probably bring the little cubs with her. This was her kill last night and we did not hear a scream."

The head of the deer turned in an awkward position. There were claw marks on the side of the deer. The big cat attacked from above and broke the neck of the deer when she landed. There would have been no cause for battle.

"We can go back and come here after dark. It would be good to give her the deer and then chase her to a new territory."

Boots and Migisi raised their family in the cave located high in the Rocky Mountains. There were many such caves, but this one became their home. The cave stretched into the mountain for a long distance. Boots could stand and walk to the stream that coursed through the back of the cave. When he first arrived at his new home, Boots found an old bear sleeping and a battle commenced when the bear realized company came to the cave. The bear eventually left to find more calm quarters, but he would occasionally return. If Boots occupied the cave, the bear would leave. If Boots headed down the mountain, the bear would spend some quiet time. Migisi told Boots the old bear lived his early life in that cave and would continue to visit until he died.

Migisi walked silently through the forest. She picked out the tracks of the big cat and saw paw prints for the two cubs that followed along. They were nearing the age where they separated from their mother. She guessed the little ones to be about fifteen months along. The mother mountain lion on the other hand grew wise in her old age. The old age for a mountain lion would be about thirteen years. Migisi thought this one to be ten or eleven years. The mountain lion showed strong signs of athleticism which disappeared around twelve to thirteen years. While she did not consider herself an expert on the big cats, Migisi's mind was almost encyclopedic when it comes to animals in the wild, especially mountain lions.

Tracks showed the lion and cubs hiding in some dense brush for a time.

"She will rest all day and when the sun begins to set, she will hunt again. That deer close to the cave will serve as a second meal since the kill is more than a day old."

"Should we be hunting her today?"

"She needs to know there is danger here for her and her offspring. Once she knows that, she will move away and that is what we want. We have enough pelts to last us, we don't need another."

Migisi led the way through the dense underbrush for several hundred yards before she stopped and turned to Boots. She talked quietly.

"We can turn back now. She has her two in that pile of brush. She knows we are here."

"I want to move to our left and go around. The meadow is not too far away and I would like to see how things are holding up there."

Boots and Migisi were away for several months visiting her family and tending to business at the trading post near the bottom of the mountain. Migisi's family lived in the Cheyenne village some distance away from their cave. Boots brought his family to the trading post years ago and his mother now owns and operates the post. His brother, August, built a blacksmith shop near the post. Wagon trains routinely make their stops at the post to resupply and have the blacksmith work on their equipment and animals. A doctor recently located near the post.

2

Boots hunted and fished in that meadow. A river ran through the middle providing a source of water for the game that lived on the mountain.

As they approached the edge of the timberline near the meadow, Boots caught notice of an animal in distress. He stopped moving until he could determine the location and source of the noise. He did not want to interrupt another mountain lion or bear. Boots walked a few steps further and used his looking glass to find the source. He spotted a fox caught in a snare. The fox wrestled with the bindings for a bit and then rested. After a short rest, the fox would commence the attempt to free the bonds.

"A Charlie Curry snare has snapped on a fox. I would recognize one of Charlie Curry's snares in the dark. See the cloth tied in the limb high up in that tree?" That is so the old man can't lose the snare."

Boots and Charlie Curry knew each other. They were not the best of friends, but as the mountain man code would go, they would be on friendly terms while having a conversation. Boots had no interest in talking with Charlie at the moment, and he turned to Migisi to indicate they were to backtrack to the cave.

"Why didn't we wait until your friend returned to check the snare?"

Migisi inquired about the riff between the two mountain men.

"Charlie and I have known each other for a long time. We trapped beaver together for a couple of years. Charlie decided to take out on his own one night, and I missed a pack of beaver pelts the next morning. When I saw Charlie at Rendezvous, I asked him about my pack of pelts. He told me that he needed them as a stake to get started. He never offered to pay me for them or anything. I thought that was a little bit of thievery. We have talked since, but only on easy terms. I think he would help me out of trouble, and I would help him, but that is about as far as that goes. I will go back tomorrow to see if he has checked the snare."

Boots and Migisi spent the evening enjoying the sounds of the Rocky Mountains. A rock slide in a nearby canyon ricocheted through the air. Animal noises stopped after the slide and resumed after a short time. Before the sun began to set, they watched eagles returning to their huge nests high in the tall trees.

"There are more eagles here now than before we left."

"It is the young keeping the old nests alive," said Migisi. "It will never stop. The eagle is so important in our Cheyenne lives. We place them very high."

It was known the Cheyenne revered the eagle. Migisi's father, Chief Ehane, wore a beautiful ceremonial headdress of eagle feathers. The headdress was considered ceremonial now that the Cheyenne tribal village did not have war plans. The headdress saw duty in the wars on the plains and those wars caused the chief to move the tribe to the mountains to enjoy peace.

Before sunrise the next morning, Boots and Migisi took off for the hunting meadow. They found the snare and the fox.

"The fox breathes. He has no energy left. He will die now."

Migisi looked over the shoulder of Boots. Questions came to his mind about the fox in the snare. It was unlike Charlie Curry to leave the fox in a snare for this length of time. Boots wondered if something may have happened to Charlie.

"We should find his camp to make sure he is alright. I have an idea of where his camp may be. We will take the trail around the meadow to the point where the tree line meets the stream. He will be camped in there."

The journey to the camp turned out to be arduous. Tree falls and heavy brush obscured the trail and Boots veered far off for a long time. He finally spotted a place where he and Migisi could rejoin the trail. Through the trees, Boots could make out the spot where Charlie set up his camp. The fire did not provide any smoke, it was cold. No movement around the camp occurred and Boots thought perhaps Charlie went somewhere to return to camp. When they were about three hundred yards from the camp, Migisi put her hand on Boots' shoulder and squeezed. She wanted him to stop.

"Look up in the tree to your right."

Following Migisi's finger pointing upward in a tree, Boots spotted Charlie. The man was tied up...his left arm stretched to a limb while his right arm stretched to an opposite limb. Both ankles were tied to opposite limbs. Charlie looked to be positioned for an execution.

"He is alive. I can see his chest move."

Charlie's clothes were removed and when they reached the trees where he hung, Boots looked up to see the man's chin on his chest. When a breeze came through the forest, the trees moved and stretched Charlie. He moaned when the pain struck his brain.

"Many were here. They raised him high in that tree. I have heard Blackfoot do this to their enemies. I have never seen it."

Migisi pointed to blood spots on the ground and walked under Charlie to look at his back. Lash marks crisscrossed his back and there were signs of dried blood caked on his back.

"We must be careful when we get him down. We will cut his ankles loose first and use those lengths of leather to tie around his waist and to the limb. That way when we cut his arms loose, we can ease him down to the ground."

Migisi nodded her understanding and started climbing the tree where Charlie's right leg and right arm were tied. Boots scaled the opposite tree. He stopped as he reached the left arm and started talking with Charlie. He told him that he would help him to the ground and that he would be safe. Charlie did not respond and Boots thought he may be unconscious.

Migisi and Boots first cut the leather straps holding Charlie's ankles to the two trees. His arms were pulled down now that they supported all his weight. Charlie is a big man weighing at least two hundred pounds. Boots wrapped the leather straps around his waist and threw them over the limb above his head. Migisi watched and when the straps were tied off, she cut the leather around Charlie's right wrist. When she finally sawed through the tough hide, Charlie fell and the straps around his middle kept him from slamming into the tree that held his left arm. Boots quickly cut the hide holding his left wrist. By this time Migisi scrambled to the ground and waited for Charlie to be lowered. She planned to ease him to the ground. Boots lowered the man and Migisi managed to get him on his back on the ground. She poured water into his mouth and he coughed some of the water up.

"That is good. I will take over from here if you will build us a camp. I can treat your friend."

Migisi learned medicine from her mother. She obtained the knowledge starting when she had her sixth birthday. Her mother took care of ailments and wounds for the village, and she became impressed with Migisi's healing powers. Migisi saved Boots' mother Mary from losing her life to pneumonia. The doctor had given up on her. That is when Boots moved his family away from the family farm.

The small campfire provided a spot for Migisi to make a poultice to spread on Charlie's back. She knew the poultice would sting like the dickens but the pain of the poultice might wake Charlie.

Boots left Migisi to tend to Charlie's wounds and he retrieved the fox from the snare. He skinned the dead fox and started drying the hide next to the fire. He thought if Charlie could recover, the pelt would help his back. Boots stopped by the old mountain man's camp and brought clothes to put on him to try to keep him from becoming chilled during the night.

Things seemed to be progressing for saving Charlie Curry. They camped for two days before Charlie started showing signs of coming awake. He opened his eyes and brought his hand to his forehead to find a wet cloth. He did not have any idea how the cloth got there. He found that he was laying on a blanket and he began to panic thinking the

Indians had cut him from the tree and were getting ready to kill him. He tried to rise and a strong hand held him down.

"Charlie, it is Boots Mc Cray. I cut you from the tree and Migisi is taking care of your lashes. Be still and I will get you more water."

Migisi gave Charlie a sip of water and he again tried to rise.

"Let him up. The medicine on his back will work better with air."

Boots helped Charlie to a sitting position.

After taking another sip of water, Charlie moved his mouth like he wanted to talk. He was finally able to say a few words.

"How long have I been out of it?"

"You have been on the ground here for two days. I don't know how long you hung from those trees."

"It was forever I tell you."

Charlie looked at Boots while Migisi tended to the wounds on his back.

"I guess I better pay you for those pelts I stole years ago. You didn't have to get me down. You could have left me in that tree. I thought I would die there."

"I am sure if it had been me in that tree, you would have pulled me down."

Charlie winced when Migisi renewed the poultice.

"That stuff stings worse than a mess of hornets. I hope it works."

"It will work, Charlie. She healed my back from an old lion paw rips so I know you will come through just fine. When you get to where you can, maybe you can tell us how you wound up in those trees."

"It was not a good day for me, I can tell you that much."

Charlie lay on his side and fell asleep.

"He will need to eat when he wakes. I will make some venison stew for us."

Migisi set about stoking the coals in the small fire pit. She rummaged in her backpack and produced a small bowl for the stew. Boots shook his head at what the woman would pack for a day's outing. He left to find a deer.

"Seems as though I remember this venison stew," Charlie said between mouths full of stew.

Charlie's memory caused him to grab the bowl and scoop stew until he scraped the bottom. He did not eat for days and his appetite returned rather vociferously. Boots looked on with his eyes large. He held a small bowl of stew and he wondered how a fellow could eat so much so fast. He looked down at his bowl and realized he had not eaten half.

"I am ready to get my camp moved. Too many people know where it is and you know I like my privacy."

Charlie grinned at Boots as he tried to stand. He handed his empty bowl to Migisi.

"That was mighty tasty, Migisi, and I thank you for all you have done for helping me."

He turned to speak to Boots.

"I am not sure how to thank you for coming by when you did. I would have been food for the birds for a long time, Boots. And, I am sorry about those beaver pelts long ago. That has been eating on me since I stole them. Maybe someday I will be able to pay you back. By the way, an old lady lion is hanging around these parts. She has a couple of babies with her. I have found that she hunts, but she gives me a wide berth. You need to be careful and watch for her."

"We know her and we are trying to move her to a different place. We can help you to your camp. You don't look too steady on your feet, Charlie."

Charlie sat on a deadfall tree log to gather his wits.

"I don't have anything to carry but these clothes I have on me. Once I get on my way, I will make it alright."

Charlie stood and turned away from camp and started toward his own camp. Boots and Migisi watched him make his way through the dense forest growth.

"He never told us how he managed to wind up in the trees."

"He must have killed a Blackfoot hunter. That is one of the ways of punishment they have." Migisi started packing for the return trek to the cave.

3

S am Baker and Rodger 'Dodger' Caldwell sat around a campfire sipping coffee, rolling, and smoking their cigarettes.

"I sure am glad I locked on to your thinking, Sam. I like it up here in the mountains. The air smells good, there is plenty of game, and I haven't seen a single sole come gunning for me yet."

"I trapped along this very river years ago before the beaver money played out. There are some of those trappers still up here, but there is a lot of country, and not many like to settle up here. The winters are long and tough, but the rest of the time is rather handy."

Rodger 'Dodger' Caldwell became a known gunslinger after a set to in California years back. His draw came fast and the gunman's reputation came fast as well. He came across the moniker 'Dodger' because Rodger never felt a bullet and witnesses saw he dodged every single one of them. Truth be known, according to Rodger, he didn't have to dodge because his opponent was a lousy shot. Another reason for the name came from a wanted poster. They were known as dodgers in California, and Rodger skipped out on a hearing that had been called after a shootout on the street of a small town. Rodger did not know about the hearing because he left town with gun smoke still floating in the air. The fellow he had the gunfight with had several brothers who were about as rough as they come, and Rodger did not want to have anything to do with them. He knew they would be laying for him at the inquest.

Sam Baker happened to be riding into the small town and met up with Rodger Caldwell.

"I need some place to hide, partner. Some men are after me and I don't want to have anything to do with them."

"Are you wanted by the law?"

Sam would not help the man if he was running from the law.

"No, I got braced by an idiot and he tried to kill me. I got him before he got me. His brothers are dumber than he was and they are going to be chasing after me."

"Follow me, I know the perfect place."

After a four-day ride, Rodger got a glimpse of the Rocky Mountains.

"We are not going to the top of that, are we? I break out in a rash over high places. I won't go up there."

"There are plenty of places that are low down where we can stay. I know the mountain fairly well. There are mountain men who know the place a lot better than me, but I don't think we will see any of them. They like to keep to themselves."

Once they entered the heavily treed forest, Rodger began to relax.

"So, you know about me, but I don't know a thing about you. Some people don't like to talk about themselves, but I need to know who I ride with in case something happens."

"I was a trapper for trade for a long time. I took to the flatlands and learned the blacksmith trade. That is hard work for anybody. I decided to give cow punching a try so lately I have been a ranch hand. I thought I might find work around that little town you were skedaddling out of like your tail was on fire. But, I just as soon find a way to live on the mountain as I had riding the range. I am not much of a cook, but there are some things I can sling together. We should have a mess of beans here in a bit. I do like my coffee, though."

When they finished the supper dishes at the little stream that ran near the camp, they spread out their ground sheets and rolled out bed rolls.

"Have you ever slept in the mountains before?"

Rodger stopped with his bedroll and looked at Sam.

"Why? Is there something I should know?"

"No. It is all the same but you will hear different noises in the trees and on the ground at night. It seems the normal noises like a possum or some other animal messing around the sound gets louder up here in this thin air. There is nothing different, it is simply a lot louder."

Rodger lay on his back and put his hat over his face. It did not take long before Sam heard him snoring. "That kind of racket will scare things away," Sam thought to himself as he punched his folded saddle blanket to try to soften the thing so he could use it for a pillow. He lay on his left side. He noticed Rodger slept with his right hand on his gun.

Stars showed brilliantly in the night sky. The moon broke through the trees occasionally and cast shadows on the ground. This is the stuff those poets back east write about, Sam thought. He checked the fire and then looked over to see his new partner snoring away. Even with his hat over his face, the racket made its way out from under his hat enough to alert things yards away. Sam slipped off to sleep. He slept soundly for a long time when he was awakened by the scream of a mountain lion. After the scream, quietness fell in the forest. Minutes later, another blood-curdling scream sounded.

Sam looked to see if Rodger woke. He saw the man standing on his bedroll, his white long johns flashing bright in the night. Rodger held guns in both hands.

"Rodger, It is alright. That is a mountain lion looking for a mate."

"That ain't no mountain lion Sam. That was a woman screaming and she is in trouble. I am going to help her."

"Rodger, don't move a muscle. Many men have heard what you heard and went to help. They didn't come back. That mountain lion is nothing to trifle with, I don't care how many guns you tote, she will win."

Another scream echoed through the forest.

"How can you sit there and let a woman be hurt like that? I have never heard such a sorrowful scream in my life."

"I can sit here because I know that scream comes from a mountain lion. She knows where we are and she is calling her mate. If you take one step off that bed roll, she will pounce on you and there will be nothing left but those white long johns. I am going to get the fire going again. They don't like the blazes. Come over here and sit next to the fire. That screaming will stop."

Rodger sat on a big rock while Sam got the fire blazing. He was shaking from the fright of sounds he had never heard. Sam put the coffee pot next to the fire to heat. When it was ready, he poured a cup for Rodger who promptly spilled drips down the front of the long johns.

"I got another pair of these. They need washing, but I can do that in the morning over at the creek. I wouldn't want to be downstream from that washing though."

Both men laughed as they began to relax from the mountain lion scare.

"I will tell you that if you hear one of those hissing or growling, there is bad danger nearby. What you heard was boyfriend looking for a girlfriend."

The next morning, Sam collected more wood for the fire. When he returned he saw Rodger dressed and getting ready to head to the river to wash his clothes and bring back a bucket of good water for coffee.

"I have the fire going so I will walk with you. There is something I want to show you."

When they were about twenty yards away from the camp, Sam pointed to the ground.

"Those are mountain lion tracks. They are very fresh and the one that left these is probably the biggest cat I have ever seen. See how the ground is pushed down? That means a big cat stepped here. There are some smaller prints and those belong to her cubs."

"Is this the one I heard with that blood-curdling scream last night?"

"I don't think it was. This looks to be a female with two young ones trailing along. She is gone now, but I will watch your back while you wash your clothes in the river."

Rodger had two sets of long johns to wash and he hung them on bushes when he finished with the chore. They made their way back to camp to make coffee.

"I am not so sure this place is for me. I don't need to be scared into yesterday by some big cat. If I can see them, I can kill them, but that deal last night was in the dark. I know you people get used to those kinds of things and I have a way to go, but I am not so sure I want to get used to something like that. Why don't we head down to that trading post you were telling me about on our way up here?"

"That is fine with me Rodger, but just so you know, we need to be careful and not set off one of those big cats."

Rodger and Sam started clearing camp.

"I don't know what we will do when we get to the trading post. That place has a reputation for the wagon trains to stop to resupply. There is a blacksmith shop there. I am not looking for that kind of work, but if we get around other folks and towns, I have to find something so I can make a living."

The two men found a wide track in the forest and they started down the mountain. Before long, they came upon a disturbing find.

"I swear, Sam. Somebody done laid down and died up here. Can you smell that?"

Rodger pulled his bandana up over his nose. Sam sniffed the air for a moment before he too pulled up his bandana.

Soon they discovered the mangled body of a man. Sam and Rodger stopped their horses and stared. The body showed signs of being torn to shreds. One arm was ripped nearly off and the other arm looked to be trapped under the body. The legs were askew. A rifle lay nearby. The man wore a gun belt with a six-shooter still in the holster. The face and head were torn up beyond recognition.

"I think I am going to be sick."

And Rodger was indeed sick. He dismounted and

walked to a clump of bushes where he lost his breakfast. He walked back to his horse and stood there looking at the remains of a human.

"What do we do, Sam? I can't get close to that, but we have to do something."

"About all we can do is see if he has any papers. Get his guns and belongings then light a fire. You are looking at a fellow that tangled with a big cat and lost. I think we have a killer on the loose on this mountain. Once they decide they can kill a human, it is like a dog learning he can kill chickens, it will take hold of the cat's mind and no human is safe up here."

Sam dismounted and joined Rodger. Hold my horse while I get the rifle and I will see what else I can get.

The carcass lay partially in the shade. Sam grabbed the rifle and moved away quickly. He handed the gun to Rodger. With his bandana pulled up over his nose, Sam put on gloves and searched the body for any papers. He removed a leather pouch, the gun belt, and some letters from the man's vest.

"I think we should move him away from the trees to an open spot. We can collect enough wood for a fire.

Rodger mounted his horse and handed Sam his lariat. He managed to get a loop around both legs and Rodger drug the man to an open area.

Neither man owned anything they could use to dig a grave.

"I think we are doing him a favor, don't you, Sam?"

"I would not want to be left out here like this for the varmints to have a feast."

After stacking sticks and logs on the body, Rodger started the fire.

"Let it burn down to coals and we will continue down the mountain. When we make camp, we can go through his papers and things. I wonder where his camp is located. I don't think that cat drug him too far."

Soon, they found an abandoned camp.

"This must be that man's camp. All of his supplies are laid out here. He built a shelter from nature around that tree."

Rodger pulled up and started looking around.

"He has been here a while. He is all set up to stay a bit. I will try to find his horse or burro while you get the fire going for supper."

"I sure am hungry, Sam. We worked through dinner time."

Sam tied the reins of his horse to a tree limb and started walking around the camp. He found a place with a little graze and water. Sure enough, a horse raised its head as he approached. Sam removed the hobbles and led the horse back to the camp. He used a trailing rope on the halter to ground tie the horse. Rodger got a fire started and searched for some cooking pans and he found a slab of bacon.

4

The aroma of freshly brewed coffee woke Boots. He slept well, but his custom of rising early in the mornings had him laying awake for some time.

"We need to track that lion. I heard a couple of calls off in the distance last night. They are active up here, and they need to move on to a different part of the mountain."

Migisi smiled at Boots. She had the same thoughts as she made breakfast for them both.

"He was looking for his mate. That call came from down the slope. I think they would be much happier if we could get them to that rocky canyon. It is not too far away and there is plenty of game there. Nobody will know they are there."

Boots and Migisi pushed hard to locate the mother lion.

They saw tracks for her and her two young ones, but they never spotted the big cat.

"Wouldn't it be good if they decided on their own to head to that rocky canyon?"

Migisi did not respond to the comment, rather she looked at Boots with a questioning face.

"Why would they do that? It is a good life up here. Rocky Canyon is covered in scrub brush. There are bears there that will swipe those little ones away quickly. No, I think we must drive them to the edge and see if they climb down. That is the way for us."

Soon the edge of the cliff began to show through the trees. Migisi grabbed Boots' arm to stop him from going further. She put her finger to her mouth for quiet.

"I saw the male go over the cliff on that ledge. If he goes down, it is likely the mother will follow. We will stop and wait."

They kept watch on the edge of the cliff that led to the Rocky Canon where the male mountain lion scampered down the side. They saw the two little ones follow a while later, but no sign of the mother cat.

"They were ready to leave their mother and she was ready to get shed of them. I have a feeling she will be having more in a few months."

Boots felt impressed with Migisi's knowledge of the mountain lion cats.

"We should move down a bit and see if we can find her prints."

Migisi led the way through the forest and the brush. At one point she stopped and pointed to the ground. Blood spots marked a trail and she followed. Boots stayed back twenty or thirty feet. After a time, Migisi stopped and waved Boots to her side. In front of her, the bushes were broken and the ground was disturbed.

"The blood led me to this. There is more on the other side. A struggle happened here. Look at the prints in the dirt."

Boots squatted and placed his hand over one of the prints. He put a finger in the indention left by a toe.

"This is the mother cat. A fight took place here, and it looks like she won. I see drag marks on the other side of the bush. Whatever she drug was heavy."

Boots went around the torn bushes and inspected the drag marks.

"This is the marks of a man. She attacked a man and it looks like he got the worst of it. You can see the marks his boots left. There is a piece of cloth it looks like from his shirt."

Boots kept following the marks until he came to a spot where they stopped.

"Something or somebody scared her away. I don't think she killed to eat, I think she killed to protect the little ones. We saw them go over the edge of the Rocky Canyon. They got away."

Migisi kept her eyes on the ground and she found more tracks.

"She got away. The big cat left the man there and ran away. What happened to the man?"

"We can find him. We have a killer on the loose, though. Keep your eyes moving."

Boots soon came upon the funeral pyre.

"Someone found him and decided on a fire. I want to find the man or men that knew this fellow."

Migisi stayed away from the ashes of the fire. The blaze burned almost everything, but there were some remains of the body. Her customs did not coincide with burning a body.

Boots walked further down from the location where the body had been burned. He found the tracks of two horses.

"These are new. I don't think they belong to the fellow the cat mauled."

After walking about three hundred yards, Migisi spotted a camp. The aroma of a cold fire filled the air. Two horses stood hobbled in a grassy area near the camp. Not wanting to approach the camp suddenly, Boots rounded one side and Migisi took the other. Except for the recently fired campfire, the place seemed to be abandoned. When they met on the south side of the camp, Boots told Migisi they should wait until someone returned. Migisi climbed up a spruce to find out if she could see any movement. She quickly crawled down from her perch. She grinned as she approached Boots.

"There are two men in the river. They washed their

clothes and left them on the bushes while they are in the water taking a bath. They do not wear any clothes."

Boots had Migisi stay behind while he went to the bank of the river. He saw two men indeed bathing in the river. One man soaped his hair and the suds managed to get into his eyes. The man grumbled as he put his head under the water. The other man laughed at the folly and continued soaping himself. The water showed soap suds floating in a circle around the two. Boots saw wet blankets, shirts, pants, and long johns stretched on bushes along the river bank. It turned out to be a washing day for the two.

When he returned to where Migisi waited, he told her that he would approach the men as they started putting on their clothes after their bath.

"Well, at least they will be clean and won't stink the place up," Migisi laughed.

"I think I recognized one of them. He is Sam Baker who trapped up here a few years ago. He left when the beaver pelt business quit. I found him to be a good man back then. I hope he has not changed his ways."

Boots kept an eye on the river bank and when the men came out of the river and started drying off, he took the opportunity to make contact.

"Sam Baker, is that you? If it is, I am a friend. If you are not Sam Baker, stop where you are."

Sam and Rodger were both startled and looked at each other with wide eyes.

"Who the hell would know your name, Sam?"

"I don't know, but they said they were friendly. So I am going to yell back."

"Yes, I am Sam Baker and who might you be?"

Their voices carried through the forest. Migisi could hear the conversation.

"I go by the name Boots Mc Cray. I live here and I am coming to the river."

By the time Boots reached the river bank, the two men were fully clothed and they were picking up blankets and other clothes from the bushes.

"My God, it is Boots Mc Cray. It has been years, Boots, and I would recognize you anywhere. It is good to see a friendly face."

They walked to the campsite and found Migisi getting the fire cranked up for coffee. Sam stopped and stared at Migisi.

"Boots, she hasn't changed one bit. The prettiest I have ever seen and I know she likes to cook. There is no better combination in this world. I wish I could find it."

Migisi smiled at Sam. She recalled several instances where Boots pulled him out of trouble and taught him how to run a trap line in the Rocky Mountains. After a brief get-together, Sam and Rodger told them of finding the mangled body of a man, and they decided it would be best to start a fire since the dead man had been exposed to the conditions.

"We didn't bring any digging tools, Boots. It seemed to be the best alternative to build a funeral pyre for the man. I managed to get some papers from his vest and his shirt pocket. He has a family in Utah. His name is Johnnie Childs. I have some letters he wrote home but never mailed. I thought we could go to the trading post and write the wife a letter and send these things to her. He tangled with a mountain lion is my best guess. He never got a shot off and his knife is clean. I think he got lazy and got surprised."

Boots and Migisi stayed with Sam and Rodger for a while. Migisi made a supper meal and they enjoyed an after-dinner coffee. Boots stood as he readied to leave.

"We are going to hunt that killer lion, but you need to be careful. Saddle up and ride down to the trading post as quickly as you can. A big cat that has killed a man will not hesitate to do it again. Migisi and I can take care of ourselves, we have done this before."

5

Boots and Migisi left Sam and Rodger and started searching for the killer cat. They moved east toward the area where the Rocky Canyon fell to the side of the mountain. Tracks led in that direction for a while but soon started heading west away from the canyon.

"It is daylight, and her tracks show that she is on the hunt. You can see where she is moving much faster than a walk."

Boots showed Migisi where tuffs of dirt settled in the track indicating a near run type print. The tracks were spread out more showing a stealth movement. The tracking continued as the day wore on. The sun began its downward trek and a campsite showed itself to Migisi and Boots. They just dropped their packs around the fire pit when they heard four shots. Two were rifle shots and two were pistol shots. They headed toward the sounds. They came to a clearing and saw a man standing over a huge mountain lion. The man wore chaps, a gun belt with two pistols and he held a rifle in his left hand.

"We heard your fire and we have been hunting that mountain lion."

"Come on in and see what Rootin' Tootin' Shootin' Billy Pines has brought down. She is a beauty."

Migisi stood to the man's right while Boots stood to the left. Billy Pines grabbed Migisi's left wrist and tugged on her.

"That is not a wise thing to do," Boots stepped closer.

"Come on woman. Get this hide off this carcass for Ole Billy Pine."

That did not happen. Billy stood a little off balance and Migisi took advantage. She used his grip on her left wrist to flip Billy Pine to the ground. He lay on his belly and Migisi quickly put her knees on his back.

Boots looked at the cowboy spread eagle on the ground as Migisi pressed both knees into his back.

"If you choose to move much, your hide may come off your carcass."

"All I wanted was for your squaw to clean the big cat for me. I think she took me the wrong way."

"You mean I threw you the wrong way? Well, I will let you up and throw you again. This time you will hit that big tree over there and hear the little birdies chirping away for Rootin' Tootin' Shootin' Billy Pine. I am not a squaw. I am this man's wife. I am Cheyenne, the daughter of Cheyenne Chief Ehane. I can skin you alive if I want to Rootin' Tootin'." Migisi emphasized his name.

Boots is laughing full-on now.

"I believe the woman wants respect out of you, Rootin' Tootin'. And if you start treating her right, she may show you how to skin that cat."

"I am some terrible sorry m'am. I am a man ready to swaller his words. I grew up different than what I said and the way I acted, and my momma would tan my hide if she knew how I treated you. Please accept an apology from Billy Pine."

Billy spit out pine needles as he felt a weight lifted from his back. He did not move out of concern that weight might return.

"Do you think I might be able to get up and stand a bit?"

Migisi left Billy Pine and started working on the big cat.

Boots held the rifle that Pine dropped when he went flying through the air.

"I guess you can get up, but be careful where your hands go. If I see you even thinking about your pistols, it will be your last thought."

"No siree. I am sure not thinking about my Colts. I don't even feel the need to touch them."

Billy began a slow process of getting to his hands and

knees and he finally stood and brushed the dust and pine needles from his clothes.

"When you are finishing slapping yourself, get over here and raise this cat on that limb."

Billy saw that Migisi started to process the cat. He looked at her for the first time and realized the big mistake he made. He turned and looked at Boots from head to toe.

"My God. I have met a real live mountain man and his wife. I should never see the day."

"Well, you almost didn't see the rest of this one."

Migisi taught Billy Pine how to take the cape from the mountain lion in record time. The skin stretched between two trees.

"I know you may think I am crazy, but after all that, I am starving."

While the skinning took place, Boots managed to bag a deer and he started frying steaks of back strap.

"Rootin' Tootin' Shootin' Billy Pine is gonna have to hang with you folks. I have learned more today that in all my years before. This is good eatin'."

After the meal, coffee boiled and all three enjoyed a cup. Darkness set in and a conversation started around the campfire.

"Migisi and I have been hunting that killer lion. You made some very good shots. All four of them were in the head."

"I heard her call you Boots, and you say her name is Migisi. But, you don't know who I am. I must reveal you are sitting with one of the greatest shooters west of the Mississippi. I travel to small towns and put on shooting expeditions. It is how I make my living."

"Why do you stay with small towns? It would seem you would make more money in the bigger cities with a shooting show."

"You are so right, but I will never again go to a big town with my show. I once put on a well-attended exhibition in a big town, and afterward, a drunk fellow challenged me. I did everything I could to stop him, and I feared he would shoot me in the back if I walked away. There were plenty of witnesses to the man bracing me for a fight. It finally came to the point where I could no longer refuse. I shot him in the shoulder. Now, I could have put one between his eyes, but I didn't. I put one in his shoulder. Everyone there agreed the man should have left me alone and the shooting was justified. There was a problem though. The man I shot happened to be the brother of the sheriff. Even with all the witnesses telling him otherwise, the sheriff grew angry with me for wounding his brother. I don't know if he wanted me to outright kill the fellow or what, but I left town. I vowed then to stay in the small towns and leave right after the show. It has worked for me. I came to the mountains to find myself. I enjoy the shooting shows, but there comes a time when I may miss striking a Lucifer that someone is holding in their mouth. I say I am ready to retire, but who knows? I plan to stay up here for a while and see if I can find peace with myself. I am too jumpy, and I want to calm down."

Billy Pine pulled a colorful poster from his bag that touted a shooting show by Rootin' Tootin' Shootin' Billy Pine.

"I might have brought a little excitement up here. There is somebody that is after me. That sheriff gave up his badge to follow me. The fellow wants me dead for shooting his brother. While I came up here to find peace, I am pretty sure he came up here to send me on to my great reward. This place may be a little crowded with me up here. I have a couple of friends trying to find me, too."

"Let me see. That would be two friends and an enemy. Is that right?"

"Yes, best I can figure. The two friends sometimes take part in my shoot-a-ramas. I almost nicked one. He held an ace of diamonds up for me to split the lead. I split the lead alright, but it was a little too close to his thumb. Ole Doc fixed him right up. The crowd thought we were on purpose with that, but I nearly shot his thumb off."

Billy gave a little six-gun twirling demonstration for Boots and Migisi. After flipping the two guns in the air and catching them by the handles, they slid into the holsters smoothly.

Boots grinned at the showman and shook his head thinking people will pay money to see just about anything.

"I do have friends, you know. Stony McGraw and Johnnie Butler will be bringing up our camping supplies.

Stony was holding that card, but you know, he is a friend and friends don't hold things against one another."

Migisi and Boots listened to Billy talk himself nearly to sleep. He pulled off his boots and put a thin blanket on the ground to sleep.

"I will tend the fire for a while. He will get cold as the night goes on. When the coals start cooling down we need to put on more wood."

Migisi watched Billy sleep. He used his hands for a pillow, and he drew his legs up to a fetal position.

"He looks like a little child sleeping like that."

Billy's hat was a big sombrero type. The hat showed signs of being expensive with a nice big crease in the crown. The edge of the brim was lined with brown material and it would stretch nearly shoulder to shoulder. The hat almost outsized the wearer.

Boots and Migisi sat next to each other while tending the small blaze. Boots continued to drink coffee. He liked coffee and he could drink a cup before bed and still fall asleep. Boots slept lightly and kept his weapons close by. This was a habit learned long ago while living in the Rocky Mountains.

Several hours went by before Boots came fully awake. He nudged Migisi to let her know he was awake. When he nudged her, she knew he heard something, or felt something and he wanted her awake also.

The coals were hot in the fire pit. Boots had a feeling

somebody is approaching the camp. He put his right hand on his pistol, and his left hand found his knife.

"Stony McGraw, how the hell are you?"

Boots came up quickly with his pistol pointed at Billy Pine. Pine sat with his legs crossed and he looked to the east. Boots heard sticks break and leaves shuffle as someone came to the camp.

"Stop where you are if you don't want a bullet in your head."

"Whoa, fellow. I am a friend. I am with Billy Pine."

"I don't care who you are, stay where you stand or you will draw your last breath. Billy Pine is here, but this is my camp and you will not come any closer unless I say so. Is that clear?"

"It is clear, but I mean no harm."

Stony felt someone relieving him of his two guns. The knife left the sheath on his back. Hands went up and down went his legs, and of course, the little derringer left his right boot. By this time, wood added to the fire causing a blaze to flare. Stony felt something poking him in the middle of his back.

"Walk carefully toward the fire. I will tell you to stop when I can see you."

"Boots, this is not necessary. This is my friend Stony McGraw. I told you he would trail me and join me up here. There is another man with him by the name of Johnnie Butler. They are both friends."

Stony walked to the edge of the light from the fire

where Boots could see him. Boots also saw Migisi standing behind the man. She waved her hand.

"You can come on in, but come slowly."

"Stony, meet Boots McCray. He is a genuine mountain man. His wife, who happens to be standing behind you, is Migisi. She is Cheyenne and it looks like she has your guns and stuff."

Migisi walked around Stony and dropped the three guns and knife next to Boots.

"Where did you leave Johnnie?"

"He was with me until that man yelled for me to stop. I don't know if he ran or what."

"He didn't run. He is asleep back in the woods a ways. He will have a knot on his head when he wakes up."

Migisi smiled at Boots.

"I think you two are more dangerous than we are. Stony here didn't mean any harm, and Johnnie is a heck of a good guy."

"Never, ever take anything for granted here on the mountain. If you do, you could lose your life. Tell your friend to have a seat and we will go fetch the other one."

Boots and Migisi fetched Johnnie Butler to the camp. Butler was getting help walking with Boots holding him on one side, and Migisi on the other. They sat him next to Stony McGraw.

"You two don't know this mountain man. This is Boots McCray and this is his wife Migisi."

Johnnie Butler held his hand to his head to ease the pain

of a knock on the noggin. His eyes grew big at hearing the name Boots McCray.

"Wait. Are you the same Boots McCray that owns the Whispering Pines ranch?"

"I happen to be the same."

Boots shrugged his shoulders and started making coffee. Everyone in the camp was awake and daylight would soon make an appearance.

"I stopped there for a bit on my way up here. I met your son and your daughter. That is one of the finest ranches I have ever set foot on. It is beautiful there. I would have stayed and gone to work there if I hadn't promised Billy I would come up here. Doesn't your mother own the trading post down this mountain? That place is going to town, Billy. There is a place to eat there called the Flapjack Café. There is a doctor living there, a blacksmith shop and a saloon has opened up there. A wagon train stopped there when I went through. There must have been a hundred people milling around that place. I have read books about Boots McCray and here I sit at his camp."

Billy Pine perked up when Johnnie Butler began talking about the little village near the trading post.

"I think we need to head for the trading post and get ready to put on a show."

"I hope you don't plan on retiring off the money you make down there. It is pretty tight at best."

"But Boots, if we could put on a show for the wagon

trains coming through maybe we could make a living without getting ourselves in a mess of trouble."

Rootin' Tootin' Shootin' Billy Pine and his entourage left for the trading post as the sun started its rise for the day.

Migisi started packing supplies in their beaver skin backpacks. She looked over at Boots who sipped the last of the coffee.

"He killed the big cat, so we can go back home now, or as soon as you get ready."

Boots looked over the edge of his coffee cup. Migisi could not see that he wore a smile on his face. He intentionally delayed his coffee drinking so she could put the packs together. Migisi did a much better job at packing and he always carried the heavy pack. Sometimes, he discovered, Migisi would put heavy rocks in the bottom of his pack as a note to be careful about what you wanted. Once he found his pack to be heavy and when they unloaded, Migisi had very little in her pack.

"You should be the man and be able to carry my things as well as yours," she laughed.

Most of the time, the packs were evenly balanced for weight even though Boots insisted on carrying more. He would sometimes carry his pack and lift the pack from Migisi. She would scout the parameters when he carried hers.

They reached their cave home. While Migisi unpacked,

Boots checked on the horses and burros. They were all ready to be fed. Their foraging area was nearly cleaned out. He took the animals to a park below the cave and they started grazing. A small stream trickled through the park to provide ample water. Boots left them in the park with the knowledge they would not roam far. He planned to bring them back to the corral at the cave the next morning.

Boots and Migisi took an early evening, both being tired from their recent journey. They put their bed on the rock slab that served as a porch for the huge cave. The stars were bright and the yellow moon shined through the trees of the forest.

Several hours passed by and Boots would drift off to sleep for a few minutes, then wake and watch the sky. This sleeping arrangement had worked for Boots for many years. In the mornings after such a night, he rose rested and ready for the day even though he caught a few winks of sleep.

That blood-curdling scream raced through the night again. He heard the scream not once, but twice. The mind of a mountain man started working overtime. "Billy Pine did not get the killer lion." Boots recognized the small nuances of the scream. He analyzed it and compared it to the one locked in his memory. It was the same lion.

Boots rose and went to fetch the horses and burros from the park. They came willingly, knowing the corral at the cave meant safety. When he returned to the cave,

Migisi handed him a cup of coffee. She knew it was the same big cat screaming in the night.

"We must go again. The big killer is still out there and this time, not far from our home."

Migisi seemed to be a little shaken this time. Nothing activated the Cheyenne woman's nerves, but this time, she seemed to be a little worried about finding that mountain lion.

6

S am Baker and Rodger Caldwell arrived at the Flapjack Café in time for the noon meal.

Ole Cookie came to the table where the two were sitting.

"Fare for the day is venison stew, vegetables, and pie for dessert. So, what will you gentlemen have?"

Sam looked up with a question on his face. Cookie smiled at him.

"What?"

"What else is there besides the fare for the day?"

"That is it. Now you can make any choice that you want. If you just want venison stew, then that is fine. If you want the stew and vegetables only, well, doggone that is fine too. If you just want pie, that is fine as frog hair."

"In that case, I would like to have the venison stew, vegetables, and pie. Do you have coffee?"

"You are in the Flapjack Café. What kind of place do you think this is? Yes, we have coffee. I will add two cups to the bill."

Sam and Rodger enjoyed one of the best meals in a long time. They both laid money on the table and when Cookie came to collect the dishes, Sam had a question.

"There is a mountain man by the name of Boots McCray who said there is a telegraph here."

"If Boots said it, then it must be so."

"You know this Boots McCray?" Rodger asked.

"Do I know him? Friend, he is one of the best men you will ever find. Boots has been there and done that twice over. He is rough and tough, but also one of the kindest men you will ever know."

Sam nodded his head in agreement.

"I worked with Boots way back when the beaver market was strong. He stayed here and I left. Where would we find a telegraph? We have some important business."

"You will find everything you need at the trading post. Mary is Boots' mother."

Rodger and Sam thanked Cookie and wandered off to find the trading post. People from the latest wagon train to stop were roaming everywhere. The saloon kept busy, looking toward the blacksmith shop, Rodger saw several men standing outside the building discussing matters. A young boy ran up the street, and Sam stopped him.

"Where do we find the trading post?"

"Follow me and I will take you there. We better hurry though because these people have bought just about everything in the store."

Sam slipped the young man a coin when they reached the trading post. Both men were surprised by the business activity. They were used to the big mercantile stores in towns, but they were not near as busy as the trading post. Finally, a break came. Mary wiped a lock of hair from her brow and motioned for Sam and Rodger it was their turn at the counter. Sam began the tale.

"We found a fellow on the mountain that had been torn to shreds by a mountain lion. We think the family would like to know what happened, and we have his wife's name and an address in California. We want to telegraph her and let her know of her husband's demise, and we need to send a packet of letters to her. We don't want the stuff, and I am sure the letters would mean a lot to her. I read one of the letters, and I got the idea they have two children, but I am not sure. His name was Russell Clinton, and his wife's name was Claudia. They live in Galt, but I don't know if they have a telegraph station there."

Mary looked sympathetically at Sam.

"If I remember right, a railroad runs through there, and they would have a telegraph. One of the wagon trains headed east not long ago had a family from Galt traveling through here. Let me try to raise the train station."

Mary left Sam and Rodger and went to the back room

where the telegraph was located. They browsed the contents of the store.

"We are in luck. The train station in Galt gave me a reply and they are waiting on the message."

Mary quickly printed out a short message for Claudia Clinton.

"The idea of this is to see if she still lives there and wants to hear news of her husband."

Mary sent the message through and told Sam it could take a day or two before a reply came back. Sam left the letters with Mary to box up to be sent once they obtained an address. Rodger inquired as to a place to set up camp and Mary directed them to a spot inside the tree line behind the trading post building. Several days went by and Sam decided to visit the trading post to see if a return telegram arrived. Mary saw him enter the store.

"I have news for you if you would like to follow me."

Mary led him to the telegraph room and she handed Sam a folded yellow sheet. When he unfolded the sheet, Sam's eyes grew large. He saw a reply from Claudia Clinton.

"Russell left. I found another man. Keep the stuff."

"Well, that was short and to the point. I guess there was no love loss between the two."

Sam folded the paper and put it in his pocket.

"I think you are right about that, and I would imagine those letters would cause more problems for her than necessary. I will keep the box if you don't want the letters."

"I sure don't want them. I guess they need to be burned or something."

"That would be a good idea. I will take care of it."

Mary ushered Sam to the front of the trading post. Several customers had entered the business while they were in the telegraph room.

"Here are Mister and Missus emerging from their bed, finally. I hope you had a good time back there while we waited."

A big burly fellow stood by the counter with a smirk on his face. Mary dealt with many different people in the trading post. The loud outburst did not phase her one bit.

"We certainly enjoyed ourselves as a matter of fact. Mary winked at Sam. What is it that you are so anxious to buy? Your price just doubled."

Sam's face flushed red from Mary's insinuation and he managed to sneak out the front door of the building before he laughed out loud at Mary's retort.

"It has been a long time since I have been with a woman," Sam thought. "But that Mary would certainly be worth considering."

Sam forgot that Mary was Boots' mother. They wandered to the blacksmith shop where several men continued to mingle and talk. They were waiting on horses and oxen to get shod before the wagon train could continue to California.

"I would be happy to stay here. My wife and children seem to be happier here than they have been in a long time.

We were hurting something fierce back home. Since we sold everything and got on the train to California, the burdens have eased. I may talk with the wagon master to see if we can pull out and try to make a home around here somewhere. There must be some land we can farm or ranch."

"That wagon master won't let you out. If you drop out you will lose all the money you gave him to get to California. He won't give any of it back. I have tried that little stunt some ways back. Even though I don't have a family, and I didn't pay as much as you paid, he wouldn't give any back. He said he needed it to get everyone to the destination."

"We had our wagon and six mules, he charged us eight hundred dollars for us to join up. I think we should get a little of it back if we don't make the whole trip."

Doctor McIntyre influenced several travelers to take up with the wagon train. He performed his duties when people were sick or injured. He felt as though he served well in his role and if he wanted to leave the wagon train, the wagon master would give a portion of his money back. It would be alright if that didn't happen because the doctor reserved plenty of money for the new start. He talked with his wife Rosanna, children Molly, Daniel, and Ellie. Mollie reached her twentieth birthday on the trip and she was anxious to get to California to find a suitor. Daniel reached his late teens and showed signs of being a strong farmer or rancher. Ellie was a precocious solitary girl. She read a lot and hoped one day to be a school teacher.

Doc Henry visited with McIntyre and told him he would appreciate another hand at the infirmary. The wagon trains were usually loaded with people who were sick, or close to being sick. He warned the new doctor that the wagon master would not return any of his money.

"Most likely, he spent everything he had at this last stop. I am guessing he will have some money left, but he will keep it close to his vest."

"I don't care, doc. I like this place and we would like to make our home here."

Doc Henry showed McIntyre several swatches of land that would be available for farming. He told him of three big ranches south of the trading post, the largest being the Whispering Pines ranch owned by mountain man Boots McCray.

"My youngest daughter read many books about that fellow. If he comes down here, she is liable to swoon at the sight of him. He is a hero in her eyes."

As predicted, the wagon master said he could not return any money.

"If you want to pull out, that will be up to you of course. If you want to stay with us to the conclusion, you can do that as well. Your money has been spent to get us this far. We don't like very much more to go, but I don't have any money for a refund."

Several friends of the family decided they too would

pull out. Many were tired of the long journey and they knew they faced much more travel. A few were still showing the excitement of reaching California and they would stay with the wagon train. The trail boss told the folks that were pulling out they must separate from the rest of the wagons.

"That is enough talk of pulling out. If you continue to dampen the ideas of people in this wagon train, it would be a shame. Separate tonight and leave these people alone."

There were two spots for the wagon trains. The one headed west rested close to the blacksmith shop for convenience. Another spot west of the trading post is marked for the trains that were eastward bound. They stopped for rest and resupply. Since they were early on the trail, their stock did not need much attention. Doctor McIntyre pulled his two wagons onto the spot west of the trading post. Four more families followed them.

Sam and Rodger spent most of the night trying to put together a plan for days to come. Sam fell asleep early in the morning. When he woke, Rodger had left the camp. His bedroll and all his possessions were gone.

"I guess he figured on something to do without me in it," Sam thought to himself. He left camp and walked to the Flapjack Café for breakfast. He used the last of his money for a hearty meal.

"Have you ever punched cows?"

Cookie started the conversation with Sam.

"I worked on ranches most of my life. The other part involved roaming around looking for work."

"There is a doc that comes in here and he is looking for somebody to help him set up a ranch. He pulled his family out of the wagon train, and they plan on settling just south of here a ways. I don't know exactly where, but he will be in here after a while and if you want to settle, I will let him know."

"That would be just fine. I like this country and would just as soon settle here as anywhere else."

Later in the day, Cookie told Doc McIntyre about the young man named Sam Baker.

"He looks to be about the same age as your daughter, so be careful with that. He camps at a spot up above the trading post. I think his partner took off for parts unknown this morning."

Doc McIntyre left the café and found Sam at his camp. After a long discussion, Sam said he would throw in with the McIntyre family. He closed down the camp and followed the doc to the family wagons. After the introductions were made, Sam helped gather wood for the cookfire.

7

Boots spotted the big tracks left by the mountain lion. The big paw prints disappeared as quickly as they appeared. Tracking in the forest is difficult because the ground cover will disguise the prints. Tree leaves move and they will sometimes blow in a breeze to cover tracks. When stepping on leaves, the track left behind may not look like a print at all. Experienced trackers learn to search the ground all around the suspected trail and also examine bushes for broken twigs. It took Boots several minutes of searching before he ran across another clue.

He came alone on this hunt. Migisi stayed back at the cave. She did not feel well when she went to sleep and they agreed for her to stay in for a few days. She put together a pack for Boots that would last him up to a week, although she did not think he would be gone that long.

Boots started the hunt well before daylight. He headed in the direction of the area where he thought the big cat roamed. As he stepped lightly through the dense brush, he thought this mountain lion is a male, and he seems to scout the area near the big park on the east side of the mountain. That park was teeming with game. The grass provided excellent graze and a stream coursed through the park to a lake. With the park's wide expanse, the tree line provided cover. Charlie Curry made his camp in the trees on the south side of the park. He picked a spot Boots used many times when he hunted with his son Little Boots. Charlie told Boots he planned to move his camp and Boots thought that now would be a good time to see if he could indeed find another camp.

After spending most of the day scouring the area for any signs of man or beast, Boots started looking for an easy spot to camp. Charlie Curry moved on, but Boots shied from that camp. While he and his son camped there several times, a superstition hit Boots. Someone else lived there for a time. He felt as though it would be like taking over someone else's cabin and that was something he would never do. Let the scent of the man rest there and look for another place.

He found a suitable spot about three hundred yards from the other camp. The tree line provided good cover and he would still be able to see activity in the park. Boots gathered wood to make a small fire and as he stacked the wood in a small fire pit, he heard growling and other noises telling him a fight is taking place nearby.

Boots followed the sounds until he found something that he had a hard time believing. A grizzly and a mountain lion were ferociously battling. He heard stories of such things happening, but Boots had never witnessed the violence. The old grizzly stood on his hind feet and took swipes at the mountain lion with both paws. The mountain lion ducked most of the swipes, but the bear connected with one and sent the big cat flying through the air. Boots thought the cat would know better than to come back for more, but that is what the two-hundred-pound lion did. The bear watched the lion regain the footing needed to make a rushing challenge. The lion leaped in the air and showed sharp teeth aimed at the neck of the bear. The cat managed to rip some hide from the bear, but the grizzly hugged the lion so tightly, it looked as though it might be the end for the cat.

The stories Boots heard always had the bear winning the battle because of the strength and size difference. The grizzly fought for food, and the mountain lion fought to protect his territory. Blood was drawn by the lion when he raked his claws across the back of the grizzly. The old bear must have felt something through that thick hide because he released his grip and the lion dropped to the ground and scampered back out of the reach of the grizzly. Two mighty creatures of the Rocky Mountains battled for what seemed like hours. Both were wounded and bloody. Limping badly, the big cat approached the grizzly low to the ground. Old grizzly swatted the cat with a powerful paw and the mountain lion went sailing once again. This time would be the last. A tree happened to interrupt the flight of the cat and Boots heard a hollow sound when the cat's head slammed into the tree trunk. The mountain lion is dead. When the cat did not make an effort to get up, the bear knew he won the battle. He dropped down to all four feet and sauntered to the cat. Boots noticed the grizzly took a heavy breath as he lay down beside the fresh kill.

Keeping a safe distance from the grizzly, Boots watched as the bear struggled to stay alive. He saw the bear seem to draw a last breath. Birds left the area long ago. There were no signs of any other varmints. Squirrels were not chattering, wolves were not present, and Boots last saw a grey fox moments before the vicious battle began. It was as though an historic battle between a mountain lion and a grizzly bear stopped time in its tracks.

Captivated by the battle, Boots lost track of time. Darkness came quickly, and Boots felt as though he just ate breakfast. He too had been caught up in witnessing the day-long fight between two majestic animals.

Building a small fire brought a semblance of reality back. The nearby stream provided water for coffee and soon the aroma of a freshly brewed pot wafted through the forest. Boots sipped from his cup as he rested on a small outcropping overlooking the battleground. He found level ground near the fire pit and rested. When dawn broke, Boots stood to see the bear and mountain lion in the same manner as the night before.

"I come bearing pelts from a very memorable journey."

Boots dropped the skins of the bear and the mountain lion on the rock porch of the cave. Migisi walked over to inspect the pelts. She unrolled the big bear pelt and turned her attention to the mountain lion.

"They both show scars and rips from a fight."

While Boots ate his morning meal, he regaled the story of the massive battle between the grizzly and the mountain lion. Most mountain men were known to stretch stories into unbelievable areas, but Boots was not one to stretch a tale. Migisi was in awe as he recounted the fight. Being a Cheyenne, the description of the events that occurred carried a special importance.

"You were chosen to see what many will never know. We will be able to make many things with this."

Migisi and Boots became quiet. The silence came as the pelts lay unrolled and they both had their minds working on the previous owner of the pelts. The grizzly attacked the mountain lion out of hunger. The mountain lion retaliated out of the protection of its territory. Both were naturally born in each. The bear pelt showed he would tip the scales at seven hundred pounds. Grizzlies have a hump on their back that is comprised of muscle that helps them dig. This grizzly's hump was enormous. He certainly had the weight advantage and as Boots saw, one powerful swipe of a clawed paw would send a man to the heavens.

Mountain lions in the Rocky Mountains grew to a respectable size. This lion weighed about two hundred pounds. Because of the way Boots removed the hide, one could see the big cat stretched nearly eight feet from tip to tip. The back of the ears and the tip of the tail were black and showed on the tawny-colored skin. Front paws the size of a man's hand showed sharp claws. The paws were unusually large and the claws retained some of the hide of the bear.

Boots tried to pull himself out of his daydreaming reverie and left the cave to check on the horses and pack burros. He and Migisi were planning a trip to the trading post soon and he wanted them to be in good shape.

During the night, the blood-curdling screams of a mountain lion reverberated in the Rocky Mountains. Boots looked knowingly at Migisi.

"The killer is still out there."

Boots brought the horses and the pack mules up from the corral to get loaded for the journey down the mountain. He looked over in the nearby park and saw several female big horn sheep grazing. With that many ewes, Boots thought, there must be a ram nearby. Eventually, an old ram walked out to join the females. He looked over his harem and grazed a bit. Soon, a younger ram appeared and walked around a bit before approaching the older, bigger, stronger ram. The young one put out a front leg to kick the old big horn who did not acknowledge the youngster. The big one walked off in a stretch.

Boots thought the older big horn looked to be about eight or ten years old and he could be venerable to a younger ram. However, this big horn did not want to lose control of the females.

Once, again, the younger buck tried to provoke the older one with a kick. This time, the older ram turned and the fight was on.

The young ram stood less than five feet away as the older buck reared up on his hind legs and charged with a powerful blow. When the two sets of horns bashed into each other, it sounded as though a gun had been shot.

Boots motioned for Migisi to join him as he sat on the porch of the cave watching a challenge from a young big horn. The first blow moved the younger ram back, but it did not deter his interest one bit. Big horns clashed and clashed with neither ram gaining benefit. One hit from the old ram put the younger one on the ground and the bigger stronger ram backed away to let the young one regain his footing. A man would have been killed by the force of these two ramming horns. Boots looked to see if the horses were settled and he saw both of them watching the battle below. Neither ram wanted to stop since both of them wanted dominance from the fight. If the old one lost, he would find another herd and challenge a younger buck. If the young one lost, he would go on his way to fight another day. Noon time came, and the two bucks were still fighting.

Boots wondered how long they could stand the hard-hitting. He saw the scull of one of the big horn rams and he remembered seeing two layers of bone that would protect the head from damage.

Sunshine started coming to an end as the two big horn sheep continued their battle. At dusk, the younger of the two decided he had enough and he turned and walked away. The old ram went after him and kicked him with his front leg to make sure the youngster did not want to fight anymore. He didn't. The old big horn resumed grazing and watching.

8

Riding horseback in the forests of the Rocky Mountains is a difficult endeavor at best. Winding trails pay no attention to the obstacles that hinder a horse. Sharp turns, narrow passages, and tree falls can stop a horse in its tracks. Fortunately, a wide patch formed making a downslope pathway stretching from near Boots and Migisi's home cave to nearly midway to the location of the trading post. From there, Cheyenne and Blackfoot tribes cleared some of the tinder brush to use the small woods for different purposes, and as a consequence, horseback riders could maneuver two abreast from the midway point to the trading post.

A two-day stop at the Cheyenne village was required so Migisi could see to the needs of her mother and father. Her father was aging and he enjoyed the trapping of his position in the village. Chief Ehane called for celebrations and festivals rather routinely. He said the activities kept the folks in the village busy and mostly happy. Migisi's mother, Nokomis, continued to reign as the healer of the tribe. She told her daughter that her father's years were coming to an end and Migisi needed to stay close to spend time with her father.

"Of course, we will have a festival tonight. Your father wants to have one every time we have a visitor. I know you are not a visitor and you still have your lodge here, but he will see it as necessary anyway. It has been a while since we had a big fire and danced."

Migisi decided she would stay with her mother until Boots returned to go back to the cave.

Boots took both horses and burros. The horses needed foot attention and the burros were hauling goods for the trading post.

Boots, Doc Henry, and August Mc Cay built a three-room log cabin near the trading post. Boots and Migisi lived in the cabin when they were not high on the Rocky Mountains. Boots enjoyed his time in the cabin. He visited with his mother, Mary, at the trading post. He put on weight eating at the Flapjack Café, and occasionally he would help his younger brother when times were busy with wagon train animals. Boots helped with the livery and corral duties.

A long time has passed since Boots came down from the cave. He entrusted the operation of the Whispering Pines Ranch to his son and daughter. Every time he visited the ranch he came away with a newfound respect for his children. Little Boots ran a good operation with the help of his sister, Ayashe, or Little One. She lost her husband before coming to the Whispering Pines, as Little Boots lost his wife Ninovan. They were running a ranch for Boots in Texas and with the two deaths, it was decided the Texas ranch would be sold and both children would come to the Whispering Pines. It was a good move for both for they managed to recover from their grief. Little Boots threw himself into the operations while Ayashe learned the business of the ranch and she learned to keep the books. Between the two, Whispering Pines Ranch grew to be one of the most respected ranches in the area.

Boots' arrival at the trading post set off a dust storm as a result of people wanting to see him and visit. Flapjack Street became busy with people moving back and forth from the trading post. The wagon train that stopped over began to get ready to travel. Another train headed east stopped to replenish supplies. Times were busy.

Boots finally broke away to take the horses and burros to the blacksmith shop and livery. He turned the burros loose in the corral and talked with August about putting new shoes on the two horses. The two horses went into stalls in the livery. He gave them both a good dose of hay and grain.

As he was leaving the livery, he saw Rootin' Tootin' Shootin' Billy Pine holding court with a crowd from the wagon train. Boots walked over to watch the show. Boots saw Stony McGraw holding a playing card at arm's length. Johnnie Butler held a square piece of wood some distance behind the card.

"You see, Ladies and Gentlemen, if I miss my mark, I could kill my two assistants. They are brave and trusting, but they know Rootin' Tootin' Shootin' Billy Pine will never miss. I will fire my pistol, which as many of you know, pistols are famous for being very inaccurate, but this time I will split the lead of the bullet by aiming directly at the card. Once the lead is in two pieces, you will hear both pieces hit the wood my second assistant is holding. Now, I must ask for complete silence because this is a very tricky shot and I don't want to get anybody hurt."

Billy pulled his six-shooter from the holster tied to his leg. He stretched his right arm out and locked his elbow. Billy squinted his eyes to look down the top of the barrel of the pistol. The front sight on the gun had been filed off. He started to squeeze the trigger when someone in the crowd coughed very loud. Billy dropped his arm and looked into the crowd to try to find the offender. The crowd remained silent.

"If that happens again, and I miss, whoever is responsible for that noise will be arrested for murder. Now, I insist on complete quiet."

This time Billy raised his arm, sighted the gun and

squeezed the trigger. The soft led bullet left the gun. The card cut the bullet and the crowd heard two pieces of lead slam into the piece of wood held by Johnnie Butler.

The crowd roared with approval.

"If you enjoyed that, come back around six o'clock this evening and you will see trick shooting by Rootin' Tootin' Shootin' Billy Pine. There is much more to come so make sure you are here."

Billy told Stony to make sure an area was roped off so that the audience that wanted to watch the show would have to drop some coins in the bucket.

The shooting demonstration would be held well away from the little village. Some enterprising boys borrowed hacks from the livery to charge for rides to and from the shooting site. Stony and Johnnie spent the day setting up a four-station shooting range for a fast-draw competition. The trick shooting would take place inside an area partitioned with bed sheets. The enclosure would allow for charging for entry, and another guise is it would block the wind from causing an errant bullet. Rest assured there would be plenty of room for spectators.

Billy Pine talked to as many would-be spectators as he could rouse. The Flapjack Café became the seat for taking advance money for the competition.

"Boots McCray, I hope you will honor us by taking part in our fast draw competition. I hear you are rather quick when you slap leather. I have promised a ten-dollar prize for first place and a five-dollar award for second. There is no third-place prize, after all, anyone that slow would probably wind up in the cemetery. It cost only a dime to enter, so step right up and put your money in."

Boots shook his head indicating he would not be entering.

"I will be part of the crowd though. We did this kind of thing at the rendezvous between beaver trapping seasons. I had all of that I wanted plus a little. You know there is always a challenge, and there is usually somebody a little faster. That is all it takes to end a career."

"I am sure we will wind down with two trying to be the fastest draw. I have appointed the trail boss and a couple of his men to make sure things don't get out of hand. I know they can because that is how I wound up here. I hope that old ex-sheriff doesn't find me here. I never saw anybody get so mad because I wounded a drunken brother. He doesn't realize that I could have killed the man, but I held up. I saved the man's life."

Billy Pine twirled his handguns the whole time he talked with Boots and other folks. It was a natural thing for him, and it seemed to keep his nerves calmed to twirl those guns. The action kept people at bay because they feared he might miss a catch and the gun goes off shooting some-body. Occasionally, Billy would ask Cookie about the time. Fast draw entrants were to assemble to hear the rules at four in the afternoon.

Billy Pine tickled the till before lining up the ten contestants.

"I will step up and demonstrate a fast draw for you, and I will meet the winner of the match in a challenge. But first, I will go over a few rules. If you break a rule, you will be disqualified. We have gone to great trouble to draw a firing line for you. The toe of your foot can touch the line, but if you step on it or over it, you will have to bow out. We are all here in an act of fellowship. Poor behavior will cause you to be removed from the competition. We have security here to see to that. There is a box at each firing station. You are to place your gun on that box for inspection. Once that happens, two contestants step forward to shoot. Once the judge determines the fastest draw, the next two will be able to have their turn. The judge's rule is final, and there will be no argument about it. We have security here to see to that. Now, I call the first two shooters to the line. Place your gun on the box, and after inspection, it will be returned to you."

Billy stepped to the line, drew his gun, and fired at the target. He hit the marked spot in the center of the target. Billy started spinning his gun forward, backward, and across the top of his hand before the pistol found its home.

The fast draw competition saw men from the wagon train trying to clear leather with their six-shooters. One man nearly shot himself in the foot. He pulled the trigger before he pulled the gun from the holster. It was clear there were no gunfighters in the bunch. When it finally came down to the last two contestants, one clearly beat the other.

"I will challenge the fastest of the contestants. Sir, it appears you have won the competition and the ten-dollar prize. Are you willing to forfeit that prize for a chance to go up against Rootin' Tootin' Shootin' Billy Pine? If I beat you, I win. If you beat me, then you win. What will it be?"

Much to Billy's disappointment, the contestant held out his hand for the ten dollars. The money amounted to half a month's wages.

The second-place finisher took his five also.

Johnnie and Stormy gathered around Billy.

"Boys, we should charge more to enter the fast draw. We have twenty cents left from the entry fee. I hoped to keep the ten dollars, but we will make it up on the shooting demonstration."

The fast draw competition finished well before the six o'clock start for the trick shooting demonstration. Billy and his entourage entered the Flapjack Café for afternoon coffees. Cookie brought out a fresh pot of Arbuckle coffee.

"You draw a better crowd than a bunch of flies, Billy. You sure have kept my place busy, and I hear the saloon next door has picked up their business, too."

When it came time for the trick shooting exhibition, a large crowd paid their way to the cordoned-off area. Families brought picnic baskets, and the young boys hauled people to the site and quickly returned to load up more folks. It was going to be an evening of entertainment. Boots walked alongside of Billy on the way to the little arena.

"Billy, I think you may have outdone yourself. I haven't seen this many people gathered in one spot in a long time, maybe forever. These people are hungry for a show and I hope they will not be disappointed."

"Why Boots McCray, ye of little faith. I have entertained bigger crowds in my day. I hope you get a front-row seat because I know you will enjoy the show."

When Billy stepped out from behind a sheet that was used as a makeshift curtain, the crowd started applauding. Billy responded by waving at the folks. He stood in the middle and drew out both guns and started his twirling. He went forward and backward. He twirled the gun in his left hand over his shoulder from behind and caught the gun in midair. He did the same to the gun in his right hand. Eventually, he stopped the gun spinning and got ready for the demonstrations. He arranged earlier in the day with a cute little girl to hand him a dime that he had provided her. When she took her seat, he invited the child's mother out to throw the dime in the air. When the coin went high in the air, Billy pulled out his pistol and fired a shot. The dime went spinning from the contact with the bullet. Everyone watched the dime fall to the ground. The woman picked up the dime and held it up for everyone to see. The bullet from Billy's gun put a bend in the dime. She handed the dime to Billy and took her seat. Billy walked to the little girl and handed her the bent dime.

"Here is a token from Rootin' Tootin' Shootin' Billy Pine."

The crowd erupted in cheers.

Next Billy shot a cigarette out of Stony McGraw's mouth. Of course, it was a self-made cigarette and Stony made sure it was a long one. The stogie went flying.

Billy told Stony to stand absolutely still. Stony had a slight belly paunch and the buttons on his vest protruded slightly. Of course, Billy shot one of the vest buttons off, much to the surprise of Stony.

Johnnie Butler made a big deal of taking off his coat and then taking off his vest. He did not want his buttons to be shot off. Johnnie held a deck of cards in his hand and at Billy's nod, he threw one of the cards in the air.

Billy altered the mechanism on his pistol so that he could keep the trigger pulled and fan the hammer. When the card went up in the air, Billy unloaded his pistol. When the card fluttered to the ground, Johnnie showed the crowd the six holes in the card.

Billy continued with his tricks until nearly dusk. The two young boys were ready with their hacks as the crowd began to break up.

One of the families that watched the shooting exhibition happened to be that of Doctor Mc Intyre, his wife Rosanna, daughters Molly and Ellie, along with son Daniel. Sam Baker accompanied the family and Rosanna noticed Molly sat close to Sam and she seemed to have eyes on him during the entire show.

"How did you like the trick shooting, Molly?" Rosanna asked.

"What? Oh, that. That was interesting."

"I notice you found something else interesting as well."

"Mother, what do you mean?"

"I think you have taken a liking to our new ranch hand, Sam. I can appreciate that because he is a handsome young man. He needs a haircut, but Sam looks to be ready for work."

"Mother, I don't know what you are talking about. Of course, I would try to size up our new employee just to make sure of things. How did you know I promised to cut his hair?"

"Molly Mc Intyre, I am your Mother. I know things. Don't ever forget that."

Rosanna smiled at a red-faced Molly as they walked toward their camp.

9

The wagon trail boss handed Billy a hatful of money.

"Take what you need out of there. You helped us out."

"I watched the show for free and I enjoyed it. I don't need any of the money."

Billy called Stony and Johnnie over to divide the proceeds.

"Boys, we did well today. As we always do, I will take half and you two divide up the other half. Oh, and here is a dollar for Stony to get his vest repaired. That was something new and it worked out very well. Thank you, Stony."

"My vest don't thank you and I have a bruised spot on my belly from that little trick. It is going to take a dollar for a new vest, but you are going to have to feed my stomach to help with that bruise."

Billy laughed and agreed to buy both Johnnie and Stormy supper at the Flapjack Café."

Doc Mc Intyre and Sam discussed finding a spread to start a ranch and maybe farm a bit to provide feed for the stock. Sam suggested talking with Boots Mc Cray.

"He owns a big spread south of here called the Whispering Pines. Maybe there is something around his place that might work for us. His ranch is well known in this part of the country."

They found Boots standing on the boardwalk of the Flapjack Café. After the introductions, Sam asked Boots if he knew of a patch where the McIntyre family might settle.

"Life on a ranch up here is not easy. There are many battles to fight, the least of which is Mother Nature. The winters are brutal and you have to be prepared for them. I do know of a place that joins mine. It was owned by a ruthless man and when he no longer owned it, a trail driver ran it for a while. That fellow got sick and died and the place has been empty since. He had no relatives and I am pretty sure you will find the house rather comfortable. I would be happy to take you there in a day or so."

They agreed to meet Boots at the trading post in a couple of days.

"He looks like a mountain man and I don't have any history with people like him. Are you sure we are on the right track with that fellow?"

"Absolutely sure, Doc. He has a reputation of being one of the best mountain men, and I found nobody that would say a word against him. He bought the Whispering Pines ranch and his son and daughter now run that. He helped another fellow settle on a ranch called the Blue Spruce which is south of the Whispering Pines. Yes, Boots Mc Cray is the real deal. I would stake my life on it."

Sam told Doc McIntyre of meeting Boots and Migisi on the mountain after finding the body of a man mauled by a mountain lion.

"We trapped together back when beaver pelts were worth some money and Boots knows the mountains like the back of his hand. He would do to ride the river with."

Doc had heard that phrase of riding the river with someone and he knew Sam vouched strongly for Boots Mc Cray.

The next morning, Boots met Doc, his son Daniel and Sam Baker for a ride to the Whispering Pines and then to the Bar D ranch. Doc rode beside Boots so they could talk on the way.

"This place I will take you used to be called the Bar D ranch. It was owned by a fellow who wanted to own all the land around it. That didn't happen the way he wanted. There was pretty much a little war over some other land, and he got himself killed. A fellow by the name of Leroy Masters took it over and he got himself thrown from a horse and he never recovered from that day. He had no relatives and with nobody to run the place, all the hands left, and now it sits empty. There is a nice big house and plenty of graze and water for cattle. Our ranch joins the place on the west side. We will stop there first. South of the Whispering Pines is a place called the Blue Spruce. An old gun hand settled there and is one fine neighbor. His name is Montana Brown."

Doctor Mc Intyre let out a little whistle when he first saw the headquarters house at the entrance to the Whispering Pines.

"That is a mighty fine-looking house and spread."

"I can't take credit for building that place. I bought it from a man and his wife. They were wanting to move to town to be closer to their children. Well, I might say that a little different. I bought the place from the wife who told her husband they were moving."

Boots and Doc McIntyre laughed.

"My son is called Little Boots. He lost his wife to illness and he brought his son Blue Sky, or just Blue out here with him.

My girl, Ayashe, lost her husband in an accident and she brought her daughter, Little Feather, with her. My wife Migisi is Cheyenne. There are reasons for those names."

Little Boots and Ayashe stepped to the front porch of the big house to greet the visitors.

"We are not staying. We stopped by on our way over to the Bar D ranch. This fellow here is fancying the idea of making a home out here and I thought the Bar D might be a good place for his family."

Little Boots stepped off the porch and stood next to the horse that Boots chose to ride.

"It would be good to have a neighbor over there. The place is ready for somebody to live there. Ayashe and I went over to the house not long ago and things looked to be fine, but a little work will need to be done."

"This is Doctor McIntyre and his son Daniel. His wife and two daughters stayed back at the trading post."

"Good to meet you, and when you need a little help getting things fixed up and ready to move in, I will come with some of our hands and spend a day or two with you to get it the way you want it."

"That would be a big help I am sure. We are anxious to get set up so we can have a place like this one here."

Doc looked around the main house. The bunkhouse was recently whitewashed. Barns and corrals showed signs of good maintenance, but what caught his eye was the stream that ran down the hill behind the house and coursed its way to the west. Cottonwoods lined the banks of the stream and Doc thought he could hear the water flowing over rocks. It made for a peaceful, restive place.

"Boots, I don't understand why you choose the mountain over this place. I would think heaven might look a little like this right here."

"The mountain is in my blood. I lived here for a long time before the mountain called me back. There is where my family lives now and I like to visit and see what they have done with the place. We need to get on the way or we could lose the daylight."

Boots did not want to talk about his desire to live in the Rocky Mountains. He grew quiet as they rode toward the Bar D ranch. He recalled hearing the loud echoing sound of the big horn bucks battling for dominance, and he thought of the battle he witnessed between the grizzly and the mountain lion. Those were just two events he would not have witnessed had he not chosen to live in the mountains.

As they approached the main gate to the Bar D ranch, young Daniel asked his father if this would be the place they called home.

"If we look it over and like what we see, I think we can live out here just fine. We can get you that horse you have always wanted. We will need to get Sam some help with the ranching part, but yes, I am thinking we may settle here."

The narrow roadway through the main gate led down a small hill to a valley. After getting through the gate, Doctor Mc Intyre stopped and admired the lush green valley. A river ran through the eastern edge. The river looked to be fifty to sixty feet at its widest point. Huge trees lined the river banks, and as his eye wandered back to the roadway, he saw the house. Trees provided shade all around the house. A porch ran from the front around to the back. The two-story building looked to be in decent shape. All the windows were boarded to protect the glass. The procession advanced slowly as Sam came alongside.

"Wow, Doc. I can hardly believe my eyes. This is a whopper if I ever saw one. The barn is a little rough but certainly fixable. The bunkhouse looks livable. I really like this place."

A tour of the house found the place to be as though someone just left to go to town.

"If we yank those boards off the windows, I declare, this place is move-in ready. We need to get back and get our wagons headed in this direction. I am beyond excited to be able to get a place like this."

"I would suggest you get over to the courthouse and get your name on the deed. I don't think there will be any problems with that, but you never know."

"Boots, I am indebted to you for bringing me to this place. You say it was called the Bar D, but I think with what has happened here, we should probably come up with something different. We should think on that a bit."

Daniel thought the trip back to the trading post would never end. He wanted to tell his sisters about their new home and he was ready to get the two McIntyre wagons headed toward the Bar D.

Doctor McIntyre got his family excited over the prospect of moving to the Bar D ranch. They decided to rename the ranch the circle M.

10

"Put him down Rootin' Tootin'."

A crowd lined each side of Flapjack Street.

Ex-sheriff Carson Sawyer swayed left to right as he stood in the middle of the street.

"Come on, you coward. Draw your gun. I am here to kill you for shooting my brother."

"Sheriff, your brother was drunker than you are. He tried to kill me. The people in town saw that I could have killed him if I wanted to do that, but I didn't. I shot him in the shoulder instead of in the head. You need to get that through your thick head. I did not want to kill your brother, and I don't want to kill you either. Go back into the saloon and have a drink on me. I am buying, but I am not drawing on you. If you want to shoot me, it will be in cold blood."

Billy Pine unhooked his gun belt from his waist and let it fall to the dirt in the street.

"Come on Rootin' Tootin'. Put him down."

"Y'all need to shut up. I am not going to shoot this man. You are all witness to me not wearing a gun. I don't want to have a gunfight, and he is too drunk for a fistfight."

Sawyer's brother watched the Rootin' Tootin' Shootin' Billy Pine show in a big town a state or two over. In his drunken mind, he thought he could out draw Billy Pine and faced off with him in the middle of the town's main street. Billy tried to talk the man down, but the fellow drew his gun and fired. The bullet burrowed into the ground a good twenty feet in front of Billy. The man raised his pistol and prepared to shoot again. Billy thought he had better end the matter, but he did not want to shoot the man dead. He wounded him in the shoulder instead. The man happened to be the brother of the sheriff, and Billy took on the run after learning Carson Sawyer was out to kill him for shooting his brother. Billy wondered how Sawyer had managed to find him in the Rocky Mountains.

Sawyer continued to sway back and forth as he muttered words aimed at Billy Pine.

Carson Sawyer had difficulty pulling his pistol from the holster. He forgot about the little piece of leather that went over the gun's hammer to keep the gun from falling out of the holster. The piece of leather did its job and Sawyer looked down to see what the trouble was. He wrestled with the leather thong and finally flipped it off the hammer. He straightened his stance and held his hand over his gun.

"We are ready now. Are you going to be a yellow belly skunk and not draw? That will be just fine with me because I will shoot you anyway."

The crowd backed away on both sides. No one knew where the bullet from Sawyer's gun might go. Suddenly, Billy saw a blur come out of the crowd and a man blind-sided Sawyer when he dove and hit him from the right side. Sawyer had managed to get the gun from the holster, and he held it in a loose grip. Of course, the gun went flying when the man hit Sawyer. They both fell to the ground and the charging man stood. Sawyer took a hit to the head during the initial contact and he lay unconscious. Billy Pine walked up to thank the man and he realized the fellow that charged Carson Sawyer was none other than Stony McGraw.

The crowd started clapping when Billy shook Stony's hand. They thought what they witnessed was a prelude to another show.

"I did not want this to happen. This man is here to avenge the wounding of his brother. He has been trailing me for a long time. I am sorry about his brother, but as you could see, he tipped the bottle too much to be out here challenging me to a shooting. I would ask some of you to help him over to the doc's office so he can be tended to. My friends and I will be leaving so he won't have anyone to be angry with when he gets well."

Billy turned and asked Stony where Johnnie held the horses. They were on their way out of town when Carson stopped Billy.

"It turned out better because of you Stormy. I hope we won't see that man again."

The three crossed the river east of the trading post and headed for the nearest town.

Doc McIntyre and his son Daniel finally found the land office in the little community west of the trading post. After an exasperating discussion with a clerk in the land office, Doc was finally able to show him the land he wanted to claim. The map lay on the counter as the clerk, dressed in a clean white shirt, played with his mustache.

"You know that land belonged to a fellow by the name of Leroy Masters. He was in here when he took over. I hear he died out there and the place is abandoned."

"That is what I have been trying to tell you for the whole time we were in here. I want that place put in my name."

"You know you are going to have to pay to have that happen. It is gonna cost you a lot of money. I hope you are ready for that."

"Just exactly how much money is it going to cost to get the land put in my name?"

"I am here to help this office make money, so it is going to cost a lot."

"How much?"

"Let me see. This paper here, the boss wrote out for me,

ought to help me answer that. I see here, five dollars, no wait. Mister, it is going to cost you ten dollars for us to put that land in your name."

Doc McIntyre pulled out ten dollars and counted it out for the clerk.

"That ought to get it taken care of. Let me get the ledger book out and I will put your name on it."

The clerk retrieved a big heavy book and dropped it on the counter. He started thumbing through the pages.

"Oh, boy, there is the place that belonged to Missus Whiting. She died a while back and her daughter is supposed to come in and sign up. I haven't seen her yet. I hope she gets her pretty soon."

The clerk kept rummaging through the book. Daniel looked at his father and shrugged his shoulders. Doc looked at the clerk wondering how to speed the man up.

"Are we going to need to get a room for this? It is getting rather late."

"You have to have patience working in this office. Haste makes mistakes. That is something my boss tells me all the time. I will get to the page in due time. Oh, here we go. It looks like your place is bound on the western border by the Whispering Pines Ranch. Did you know that ranch is owned by a real live mountain man? Yes, sir, his name is Boots Mc Cray. You can see it right here. And then, on south on the west border is the Blue Spruce Ranch. You have no southern boundaries and there is nothing to the east. You own a big spread of land."

The clerk bent over to look at the form to change ranch ownership. Doc McIntyre figured there would be a need for his name and the brand for the ranch. He put a piece of paper with his name on it next to the clerk's hand.

"Now that is certainly a handy thing to do. I would have been asking you all this and sometimes my hearing is not so good. Here you have gone and wrote it out for me. Did you know a lot of the folks that come in here can't read or write? But you got it all figured out in a hurry."

The clerk set about filling out the deed papers and Doc McIntyre and Daniel left the land office in time to get to the diner for supper. After their meal, they walked out of the diner and stood on the boardwalk. A crowd began to gather in front of the sheriff's office.

"Father, is that Rootin' Tootin' Shootin' Billy Pine over there?"

"I think it is. I thought they left the trading post headed in the other direction. They must have changed their mind."

They walked to where the crowd assembled and watched Billy Pine show off his gun spinning much to the thrill of the crowd. He ended the show when Stormy threw up a card and Billy shot a hole in it. Of course, another fast draw competition would be held before the trick shooting show. This time it would cost fifty cents to enter. Billy must have learned his lesson with the ten cent entry fee.

Eager to return to the trading post and get the wagons

headed to the new Circle M ranch, Doctor McIntyre and Daniel wasted no time mounting and riding.

Daniel grabbed the deed paper from his father and ran to his mother and sisters.

"We got it! We got it! We own the Circle M ranch, let's go. He had forgotten his mother and sisters had not seen the ranch and they only knew what Doc and Daniel told them about the place.

"You make this place sound like a piece of heaven, Daniel. We haven't seen it yet and now we own it?"

"Yes, we own it."

Doc McIntyre stepped between Daniel and his mother and took the deed. He folded it and put it in his pocket and he hoped Daniel would be able to calm himself.

"We need to go to the livery and buy me a horse and saddle. Can we go right now?"

"Son, I think the important thing for us to do right now is to take your mother and sisters to see where we are going to live. They need to see the place for themselves."

The two wagons were readied. Sam drove one wagon with Molly sitting next to him and Doc drove the other with Rosanna and Ellie sitting next to him.

11

Tell me all about our new home, Sam. Isn't this just the grandest thing that ever happened to us?"

Sam used the ride to enlighten Molly about her new home.

"The house is big and there are plenty of rooms for each one of you. We didn't get to see much inside because the windows were boarded. We will take those boards down first thing."

Doc drew the first wagon to a stop at the gate to enter the main grounds.

"Oh, Bill. There are people already here. We must be at the wrong place."

Doc spotted Little Boots and Blue who were removing

the boards from the windows. They stood on the front porch and waved the travelers in.

"That is Boots Mc Cray's son and grandson. They offered to help get things ready for us. I didn't know they were coming on over, but it is for the best to meet them now."

Doc flicked the reigns for the mules to pull the wagon through the gate. He pulled up next to the big porch and Sam followed behind.

After the introductions were over on the front porch, Doc opened the door to the house and waved Rosanna, Molly, and Ellie to come inside. All three of the females put their hands to their mouths as they surveyed what was to become their new home.

"Mother, everything is in its place. The furniture is perfect. I looked in that room and there is a study in there with a big desk with paper on it. It is as though somebody just left."

"William, I am simply speechless. This is fabulous and it must have cost a fortune."

"Ten dollars, Mom. Yep, that is all it cost. Ten whole dollars."

Doc laughed at Daniel's excitement.

"That is what it cost to get the deed paperwork done. Let's look around."

Ellie came bounding down the stairs.

"I have my room picked out. Come on, Mother, and let me show you."

The tour of the house began.

Doc stepped outside and stood on the front porch. Little Boots came up the steps and stood next to him. We are getting the mules brushed down and grained. There is plenty of grain in the barn, but you are going to need more. When they finish with the mules, the boys will come over and help unload the two wagons. What we don't get put in the house, we will sit on the porch here so you folks can take your time with it. You sure have a nice place and we are glad to have you as a neighbor. Leroy was a nice man, but he kept to himself and we hardly saw him. I know Ayashe will be happy to have lady company. She wanted to come over today, but I convinced her to wait until tomorrow so she can help you in the house."

Little Boots headed for the bunkhouse where Sam had just pried open the door.

"We haven't been in here yet, Sam. I don't know about this bunkhouse."

When they entered, there was a musty smell from being closed up. Sam saw a hand pump on a dressing table. A large bowl sat under the spout. He grabbed the pump handle and started working it up and down and soon clear water gushed out of the pump into the basin.

"I have never had water in a bunkhouse before. This will be kind of nice."

" Leroy Masters required his ranch workers to wash their hands and face before going to the big house for meals. That is why there is water in here. I think you need to put the bedding on that line out there and let it air out a bit. These windows will open and a breeze through here would surely help things."

The windows went up and Sam wrestled with the bedding until he had everything hung out on a line behind the bunkhouse.

"We have a little air coming through here and things are beginning to feel a little better. I am interested in looking at the pastures and the rest of the layout of the place. Little Boots agreed to take Sam on an inspection ride.

"There are no fences out here. It is important for neighbors to be neighbors. Your cattle will wind up on our place, and ours on yours. As long as they are branded there should be no problems. We can agree on a time to divide them up. There are some Bar D cattle left on this place. They will be wild, but we can help with a roundup. I would suggest you do that soon so you can put your brand on and get an idea of the number you own."

Sam was impressed with the advice Little Boots gave. He would be a big help to get the ranch started.

"I imagine Leroy left his books in order before he died. Doc will probably find them in that big desk in the study."

Rosanna, Molly, and Ellie were through with the tour and they started putting things in their place. Daniel would open a crate on the porch and the ladies would take the things inside and put them where they thought they would belong. Many of their belongings have not been seen since they were packed for the trip in Missouri.

Doc continued to look over the grounds, the barn, and the corral. The mules were taken out of the stalls in the barn and placed in the corral. Water was pumped into a lengthy trough. The corral was larger than Doc expected. He leaned on the top rail and gazed to the south and east. Sam and Little Boots walked up to join him.

"Doc, Little Boots has agreed to take me out to show me the land as best he knows it. He tells me the previous owner kept good books for the place and they would be worth looking at to get an idea of how the ranch was run. I would like to see those books. We need a map of the place, and we need to get an idea of the number of cattle, ranch hands, supplies, and other things that he had to buy. I am thinking we should start slow and build the ranch up to a nice money making size."

"Sam, you do what you feel is best for the Circle M. We have the funds to run the place. Rosanne and I are looking forward to resting a while, and then enjoying a sort of retirement. In other words, we are going enjoy watching you work."

The men laughed at Doc's comments.

"That will be just fine with me as long as you are around so I will have somebody to talk to about the ranch. Little Boots and I will look for a map in that desk if you don't mind."

"Sure, go ahead. I am sure the women folk are busy getting things out of the wagon and into the house. I have a little surprise for Molly in the bottom of one of the wagons. I had the floor built over it so I know she has no idea about it."

"If they get everything unloaded, just leave the wagons where they sit and I will see to getting them moved. We can get that surprise out of there before the wagon goes to the barn. We are going to need to take one of them to the trading post to load up a few supplies."

Sam and Little Boots found a map that described the boundaries of Circle M. Sam whistled at the size of the ranch.

"We will not be able to see all of this in one day. I want to look at the land that we can see today, and maybe after things get settled we can go to the edges of the place."

The two men rode to the eastern boundary of the ranch and along the way, they saw about a hundred head of cattle in a small canyon. The canyon had plenty of graze and water so they were content to stay there.

"It will be easy to get them out when we need to round up. I bet there are more on this place than we know."

Little Boots agreed.

They arrived at the headquarters house before the sun started to go down.

One wagon had been emptied and the other had a scattering of things left on the floor.

"The empty wagon is holding the surprise. I will tell you what it is. Molly learned to play the piano beautifully. I knew we couldn't take a piano on our trip, so we had her learn the pump organ. The pump organ she learned to play is hidden under the false floor in the wagon. Rosanna knows about the surprise and when we get ready to bring it out, she will keep Molly busy in other parts of the house while we put it together in the parlor."

Sam set about to get the boards removed. He smiled at the beautiful woodwork on the organ, and he thought about Molly's hands on the ivory keys. Doc poked Sam with his elbow.

"Are you through drifting, Sam? This needs to come out a piece at a time and we will make the assembly in the parlor."

Sam was brought back to reality and the task at hand. His face reddened at the thought of being found out about daydreaming about Molly, especially caught by her father.

Doc let Rosanna know they were ready to move the pump organ and she took Molly and Ellie upstairs to work in the bedrooms.

The pump organ was heavy and required Little Boots, Blue, Doc, and Sam to lift the heaviest part from the wagon. Once all the pieces were inside, Doc knew exactly how they went together. The sun went down and the house lanterns were lit. The pump organ glowed after the dust was wiped off with oily rags. Doc nodded to the three men the job was done. He called to Rosanna to bring everyone to the parlor. Molly followed her mother into the room and she suddenly stopped when she saw the pump organ.

"Father! How on earth did you do this? This is the very

organ I learned to play. I know because there is a tiny notch in the key of c."

Molly had tears in her eyes.

"There is nothing more that will make this place home than to hear you play. Have a seat. We are ready for some music."

Molly picked up a sheet of music from an old hymn and sat on the bench. She pumped the pedals and pulled out several stops. She paused for a moment with her hands above the keys and then started with the hymn Rock of Ages.

Sam seemed to be in a trance as Molly played the organ. Doc sat next to him. Rosanna and Ellie stood beside the organ and watched Molly's hands move expertly across the keyboard.

During the impromptu recital, the canvas and bows were removed from the wagon with the false bottom and two of the rested mules were harnessed and hitched.

Sam and Little Boots stepped up to the seat of the wagon, Sam carried a list of supplies needed and Doc gave him a money pouch to pay for the goods. They would take the wagon to the closest town to get the supplies from a mercantile store.

12

They took the well traveled road after passing the trading post. They met an eastbound wagon train with thirty wagons trailing the lead wagon. Much to Sam's surprise, he discovered Rootin' Tootin' Shootin' Billy Pine, Stony McGraw, and Johnnie Butler traveling with the train.

"These people wanted to see a show and I told them they could see one if they stopped at the trading post. That is where we are headed."

Billy Pine was his happy go lucky self and he was enthused about the prospect of being able to put on another show at the trading post.

"I sure like that country. I hope old Carson Sawyer is gone from there. We plan to stay there a while."

During the first night, the eastbound wagon train

stopped at the trading post, the Rootin' Tootin' Shootin' Billy Pine show was a big hit. Most of the travelers were happy to leave California because they fell on hard times. Some were simply unhappy to be away from their homes back east and those folks seem to have money. The hat was filled with money by the time the last bullet left Billy's gun. The three men gathered to divide up the evening's takings. As was their agreement, Billy took half the pot, and Stony and Johnnie took the other half. When that was done, they walked to the Flapjack Café for supper.

"We keep this up, boys, we will be able to build a place for this show, and maybe even build us a place to live. Now wouldn't that be something?"

Billy and his partners sat at a back table in the café. While they waited for their food, people were stopping by to express their pleasure in watching the show. Billy was beginning to get the feeling of becoming some sort of celebrity.

Cookie loaded up plates with beef steaks, mashed potatoes with cream gravy, and fresh vegetables.

"Y'all dig in. This is on the house. That fellow up front there paid your bill."

Billy looked up to see a man dressed in a suit. He looked at Billy and saluted with two fingers to his forehead.

"You three are good for my business. I think the saloon next door has been a little busy too. Why don't you think about staying here and putting on those shows you do for the wagon trains coming through? We have word there is one coming through in a day or so. They are headed to somewhere in California and they are coming from Illinois. Now if there is anybody that needs entertainment, it would be those folks. I know you have to make some money to stay alive, but there should be enough work around here to keep the three of you busy."

"Work you say? Rootin' Tootin' Shootin' Billy Pine don't do no work. It is me and Johnnie Butler here that do all the work. All he does is twirl those guns of his and people pay money to see it."

Everyone laughed at Stony's remark.

Boots sat at the adjoining table and looked over at Billy.

"You know that fellow that was after you when you were here before is still around here."

Billy raised his eyebrows.

"Carson Sawyer I believe was his name."

"Yes, that is the old ex-sheriff who came looking for me because I wounded his drunken brother. I checked with the sheriff when I was in town and there is some paper out on him for shooting somebody. The sheriff said the rumor had it that he shot somebody that looked like me. I don't know, I just hope he is caught before he does anything stupid."

A commotion commenced on the boardwalk in front of the café. Boots stood and walked to the front door. He put himself in the way so that nobody could get around him and go out. Boots saw a fight between two men. One of them he recognized as Carson Sawyer. When the two separated to start the fight up again, Boots recognized Doctor William McIntyre.

"You keep your filthy hands off my daughter."

"I saved her life you ungrateful cur. She was about to get run over by that horse pulling that wagon. She would have been dead for sure."

Sawyer bent slightly at the waist. He had taken a vicious punch to the belly and he felt it. He held on to Doc McIntyre's youngest daughter Ellie.

"Ellie Mae, get over here beside your father."

"I can't. He won't let go of my dress. I don't want to rip it."

Boots had seen enough. He walked out on the boardwalk to stand in front of Sawyer.

"Let the girl go."

"You go to hell mountain man. You don't have a dog in this fight so get out of the way."

Boots did not like for folks to give him directions and Sawyer's last word was met with a pounding fist in his left jaw. He was hit so hard that he tumbled off the boardwalk into the street and lay there with his arms and legs spread out. He had let go of Ellie's dress and the child stood next to her father who was rubbing his right fist with his left hand.

"Somebody needs to tend to the man. I think he has been knocked unconscious."

Doc Henry stepped out from the crowd and kneeled beside Sawyer.

"Yes, he is out like a light, and he is going to need a little dental work also."

Doc Henry held up several teeth that were on the ground.

"I will be happy to take him to town to see the dentist when he wakes up."

Everybody turned to see the speaker was Billy Pine.

"We will stop by the sheriff's office on the way to see the dentist."

Boots' brother August told Billie he would pull a wagon up and they could ride together.

"I will make sure that man makes it to the sheriff's office."

Carson Sawyer began to wake when they put him in the bed of the wagon.

"I will keep an eye on him while you drive the wagon to town."

"I know the way, but I have never driven two horses before."

Billy flicked the reins and the horses took off to a steady run. August reached for the reins and slowed the horses to a walk.

"I am pretty sure we will get there if you keep them to a walk. These horses have won races before and they like to run so you will need to keep a tight rein."

Billy grinned at August as he held the reins.

"It was sure fun there for a short time. I kind of

wondered if this old wagon would hold up. I am sure glad it did."

Billy got a teaching about the Charter Oak Wagon as they continued to town. Occasionally, August would look over his shoulder to see that Carson Sawyer was still with them. He had curled up on the bed of the wagon and August thought Billy ran over every rock in the road. When the wagon wheel hit a rock, it shook the entire wagon and Carson would moan. It seemed as though there was a constant stream of moaning coming from the back of the wagon and August thought they could not get to town quick enough.

When the wagon pulled up in front of the sheriff's office, Billy jumped down and went inside.

Sheriff Riley was surprised to see him standing at his desk.

"Billy, I thought you had moved on. Don't tell me that you have come back here looking for a place to live."

"No Sheriff, I bring tidings from an ex-sheriff by the name of Carson Sawyer."

"I think I have something on that fellow."

Sheriff Riley produced a poster for Sawyer with a two hundred fifty dollar reward if brought in alive.

"I got him, Sheriff Riley. He is in the back of that wagon yonder just waiting for you."

Sheriff Riley looked over the sideboard of the wagon to see Carson Sawyer. He had blood on his face and he did not look to be in the greatest health.

"Are you going to tell me what happened to him or do I have to guess that you two got into a fight."

"That is not it, Sheriff. August up here will vouch for the story I am about to tell you."

Billy told the story as best he could because he was inside the Flapjack Café, his way being blocked by Boots McCray. When he got to the part about Carson being bloodied, Billy stepped back and put both hands in the air.

"I did not touch the man. Boots McCray retrieved possession of the young girl with a swift fist to the jaw. Doc Henry says he lost a few teeth and the dentist needs to have a look at him."

Sawyer began moaning again.

"No dentist. I won't have no dentist in my mouth. I will get by with what teeth I have left, but no dentist."

Sheriff Riley shook his head at Sawyer.

"You are in my care and I have to take responsibility for you. I am getting a doctor over here, and if he says you need a dentist, you will get a dentist if I have to handcuff you to the bars in that jail cell. Now get up from there and march yourself into my office like a man. Quit wallowing in these people's wagon. Oh, hello August. I just now noticed you here.'

Carson Steward climbed over the sideboard of the wagon and made a move as though he planned to run. Sheriff Riley put out a boot and tripped him up. Steward landed on the boardwalk in front of the jail. The sheriff motioned for his deputies to carry old Carson to his new cell.

"After you lock the door, I want you to run over to the doc's office and tell him we need him over here. The county will be paying."

The sheriff noticed Billy kicking a dirt clod around in the street like a little child.

"Billy, come on in and I will get the paperwork set up for the reward. He is Carson Steward and he is barely alive, but he is alive. It will take some time for the money to come in and I will bring it to you if you will wait at the trading post."

Soon August and Billy were on their way back to the trading post.

13

How is little Ellie Mae fairing? I know things like what happened to her can kind of be a bother sometimes."

Boots looked at the little girl and he saw no signs of being worse for the wear. She worried with a small tear on the sleeve of her dress.

"I am fine, Mister Boots. That man didn't scare me. I was ready to give him a kick between the legs like Mother says I can do if I have to. He tore my dress a little, though."

Doc McIntyre smiled at Boots over Ellie's comments.

"Ellie is rather proud of that dress she and her mother made. It is the only dress she will wear. She normally wears pants and a shirt, and I know that Steward would have been put on the ground by this young lady had you not stepped in when you did. Ellie Mae is like her mother. Nothing fazes her."

Boots saw his granddaughter, Little Feather, riding her pony on Flapjack Street. Little Feather saw Boots standing in front of the café with a man and a young girl. She reined her little Indian pony to a stop and slid off the horse's back. Little Feather did not use a saddle and there was no brace and bit. The pony was trained to feel the pressure of Little Feather's' knees to know which direction to go. An old cotton rope served as a makeshift halter for stopping.

As Little Feather stepped up on the boardwalk to talk with her grandfather, Boots saw about a dozen Cheyenne braves walking their horses toward him.

Ellie Mae's eyes grew big for the second time this day as she spotted the Indians. She turned to Doc McIntyre excitedly.

"Father, look, there are Indians. Are we in trouble?"

Little Feather, who was just a little taller than Ellie, turned to the young girl.

"They are with me. Don't worry, these are my people and they are good people."

Boots had an idea why a dozen braves were accompanying his granddaughter.

"Do you have words for me Little Feather?"

"Yes. Great Grandfather is low and they have been sent by Grandmother to take you home to her."

Soon, Ayashe, Little Boots, and Blue rode up behind the

Cheyenne Braves. One of the braves, an older man, urged his horse forward. Boots stepped forward.

"Harkahoma, you have come for me?"

"The girl rides fast. We are here to take you home."

Harkahoma is Chief Ehane's brother. Many times he took it upon himself to take care of unenviable jobs for the tribe. Chief Ehane called on Harkahoma's wisdom during the meetings of the elders. It has never been questioned about how Ehane became chief and Harkahoma became happy in the role he served. Chief Ehane proved his worthiness as chief during the tribal wars on the plains. Chief Ehane moved the village to the mountains where they enjoyed times of peace.

Over time Harkahoma proved himself to be a man of few words. Boots nodded acknowledgment and walked to the livery to get his horses and burros. He had stored his packs for the burros in the tack room of the stables. He saddled his horse and led Migisi's horse. The two pack mules were trained to follow and a small rope tied to the back of the saddle on Boots' horse was all that was needed.

Little Feather had stayed behind and wanted to talk with Ellie.

"Your grandmother is a princess, right?"

Ellie was in awe of Little Feather and the fact her grandmother was a Cheyenne princess.

"My grandmother's father is Chief Ehane. She is a princess, but she doesn't really care to be called that. Her name is Migisi and that is what she likes to be called. She stayed with her mother to help take care of her father. My grandmother knows medicine like your father."

The two girls continued to talk until Boots joined the rest of the people to begin the trip to the Cheyenne village.

"I will have to stop at the trading post. There are some things I need."

Little Feather grabbed the mane of her pony and easily swung her right leg over the back of the horse. When she finished mounting she looked at Ellie.

"We must go riding. When I come back, I will bring you a pony like mine."

The pony Little Feather sat astride was mostly white with brown on its rump and sides. The mane and tail were of brown hair.

Ellie smiled and waved goodbye to Little Feather as the girl kneed her horse to get moving. She followed Boots and rode in front of her mother and uncle and her cousin. The dozen Cheyenne braves followed some distance behind. When they reached the mountain, the Cheyenne braves would be hard to find. They would fan out on both sides of the McCray family. Several would scout up front while the rest made their way through the forest. Harkahoma brought up the rear of the entourage.

After about an hour's travel, Boots saw another group of Cheyenne braves ahead. This bunch contained more than fifty braves. Boots turned in his saddle to see Harkahoma riding up to talk.

"There is word danger is in the trees. We are here to make sure your people get to our village without harm."

Harkahoma stopped his horse while the McCray family continued up the wide track that led up the side of the Rocky Mountains.

There were no sounds in the forest. The presence of people caused the birds to leave. The only thing that could be heard is the snap of a twig as a horse misstepped. When they reached the village, many of the braves brought in wild game taken on the trip. Elk, deer, and moose were the fair and there would be plenty for everyone to take part.

Migisi and Boots had a lodge located next to the chief. Boots took his family there and found Migisi talking with her mother. She stood and greeted everyone with a hug.

"I am glad you are here, and our children and grand-children are here. We can all sleep in this big lodge."

Migisi's mother appeared frail, more so than when he saw her just a month ago. She was a strong woman and she commanded knowledge of medicine that doctors could learn. She passed that knowledge to Migisi and she trained some of the other women in the village. She told them that one day she would need them to know everything to help her get well. Her name is Nokomis or Daughter of the Moon. Today, her face looked drawn. Migisi helped her stand and her mother leaned into Migisi for support. Nokomis seemed happy to see Migisi's children and grand-children. After greeting them, she turned to Boots.

"The great Chief Ehane will want to see you. He is

sleeping now and when he wakes, I will take you to him. We must get ready because the Great Spirit will soon visit and take Ehane with him when he leaves. The Chief is ready. He told me so. We are not ready, but it will happen."

Boots nodded to the wise old woman. He helped her to return to her seat on the floor of the lodge.

Red Feather pulled the door cover open and looked inside the lodge. He looked everyone in the eye and settled on Boots. He motioned with his head that he wanted Boots to join him outside the lodge.

"I like that you are here. My sister misses her family, and we will soon have hard times to get through. I am with my father most of the time, and he has prepared me and the elders so that I might step in as chief one day. That day, he tells me, is coming soon. I do not want to be chief unless the people want me to lead them. If they do, I will lead them as my father led them. I want you to sit in our circle of elders. You are needed here. I know your place is up on the mountain, and you must live there. But sometimes you bring Migisi and we can sit and talk."

This is one of the few times there would not be a festival upon the arrival of Boots and his family. With Chief Ehane lying near death, the focus is on him and his departing with the Great Spirit.

After midnight one night, Nokomis opened the flap on the door to the McCray lodge. Migisi rose to meet her mother, knowing what had happened.

"He is gone, my child. We talked before he left. He

wants Red Feather and his daughter Migisi to rise to take care of the village people. He was afraid there will be trouble when he is gone and you and Red Feather must be strong and end the trouble."

Two old wise men were cantankerous members of the elder circle. Both wanted to become chief, and they knew the order of things would have Red Feather take over from his father. Red Feather had been acting on Chief Ehane's behalf for several months since the chief became sick.

While Nokomis talked with Migisi, the death dance started in front of the chief's lodge. Red Feather had awakened the village with the news of the death of his father. Migisi quickly dressed in her traditional Cheyenne wardrobe. It was a wardrobe to adorn a Cheyenne princess. Everyone in the McCray lodge woke with the busyness taking place. Blue Sky and Little Feather had never seen their grandmother dressed as an Indian princess. This being their first visit to the Cheyenne village, both Blue and Little Feather found the people to be very friendly and welcoming. They felt as though they belonged to a very large family.

14

Billy Pine, Stony McGraw, and Johnnie Butler decided to settle in the village near the trading post. A westbound wagon train with over a hundred wagons circled up on pasture land southeast of the post. People began milling everywhere. The blacksmith shop and livery boomed with business. Some of the more well to do families would stay the night in the Kit Carson Hotel as a break from the long travels. It provided a nice place to have a good bed. The saloon saw more business, and of course, the Flapjack Café stayed packed with people most of the day. Cookie enjoyed the business, but he complained constantly about exhausting his supplies of beef and other stores. He filled a smokehouse with beef in anticipation of the wagon train arrivals. Those who knew Ole Cookie were well aware of the complaining, but they were also well aware Cookie would never run short of food.

Mary worked out a deal with her son August for the loan of a wagon to go on supply runs. During busy times, the wagon would make up to two trips a week. Mary hired two young men she trusted to make the runs for her. Occasionally she would employ Stony and Johnnie to make the runs when the two young men were called to other duties. Billy Pine spent his days hawking for folks to attend the gun shows. He discovered the two young men that worked with Mary could fiddle and play guitar. The wagon trains usually had some infrequent entertainment, but Billy Pine planned to put on an extravaganza with singers, players, and a trick gun shooting. His efforts were so successful the first round of performances would take two days. He put on a Friday night show, a matinee Saturday afternoon, and then the premiere, according to Billy Pine, performance happened Saturday evening.

The reviews came in positive for Billy. He and his two cohorts did make money and they would probably have a repeat when a big wagon train came through. Most of the time, however, the shows were on Saturday evenings due to the smaller wagon trains. People were pouring into California by the thousands and Rootin' Tootin' Shootin' Billy Pine saw no end to the opportunities to perform his shooting skills for folks.

The entertainment grew a good reputation, and the wagon trains sometimes veered off their given course to be able to stop at the trading post for the folks on the train to see the show. An eastbound wagon train landed at the trading post while a rather large westbound wagon train circled in the usual spot southeast of the trading post village.

Billy saw the potential for premiere entertainment when he learned there were several soiled doves on the train headed east. They left California for a better life.

Rachael Drake invited Billy for an evening meal. He learned Rachael helped the women pool their money to buy a wagon and pay for passage back east.

"Rachael, I put on a trick shooting gun show. We have some folks that play musical instruments and some people try to sing. Do you think you ladies would be interested in baring a knee for some dancing up on the stage? The dancing must be tasteful and there must not be any idea of the ladies' previous employment. We have women and children attending the entertainment. It will be a good first start to getting on the way to a good future."

"I don't know, Billy. Most of the girls are looking for a husband to settle down with. But, let us talk."

Eventually, Billy's suave demeanor convinced Rachael and seven more ladies to participate in the show.

The musicians gathered to hear Billy's idea of how the show would proceed. The fiddle players became excited.

"I think we could use a dance floor. We can put on a show for the ladies to dance, and then have us an old fashion barn dance, or maybe a street dance."

When the time came for the Friday night show, word spread like wildfire about the lady dancers being on the big stage. You boys and teenagers crowded up to the front as adults laughed at their eagerness to see something they had not seen before. Nothing was said about the women's previous employment, it was simply announced the musicians would be accompanied by dancers on the stage.

Doc McIntyre took his family. Of course, Mollie sat with Sam and they were both enjoying the entertainment. Part of the entertainment was the young boys close to the stage. They caught the eye of the dancers and they put on a show for the boys. Sometimes a skirt might flip a little high and show a thigh, but mostly the dancing remained rather tame.

Billy prepared himself for complaints, but there were none. Most of the comments about the entertainment came on the positive side. Of course, most of those comments came from the men folk. While they did not express their displeasure with the women dancing, several of the wives wore a frown until the dancing act ended. Billy told the crowd the musicians would play longer so they would have a chance to cut the rug. Waltzes and squares sounded through the early evening. Billy's trick shooting show took place on the stage and the crowd enjoyed the shooting.

The next day, Billy went to the trading post for supplies.

"Here is a list of things I need, Mary. I am running out

of lead and gunpowder and I need that worse than anything. But, I have a few other things on there as well. If you can tell me how much I owe, I will pay you now."

"I don't have any idea how much this list will cost, Billy. If you are worried about not having your money when the supplies come in, leave some money with me and I will keep it in the safe."

Billy handed over a bundle of folding money and Mary had him follow her to show him the money would be safe. When they returned to the counter in the trading post, they were surprised to find Sheriff Riley.

"Billy, I am glad you are here, and I don't have to go looking for you. I have your reward money for the capture of Carson Sawyer."

He handed Billy a fat pouch of money. Billy promptly handed the pouch to Mary.

"Could you please keep this in that safe for me?"

Mary agreed and went to store the money away.

"Now, I have some not so good news, Billy. Carson Sawyer escaped. Marshals were taking him to stand trial and I don't know how he did it, but he got away from them. It happened a long way away from here, but I will tell you he has it in his head that he has to kill you. I will let you know if he is caught again, but until that time, watch your back."

Sheriff Riley left through the front door as Mary returned to the counter. She saw Billy's pale face.

"You look as though you have seen a ghost, Billy. What did the sheriff have to say?"

"He said that Carson Sawyer got away from the federal marshals and he will try to come here to kill me. I am not scared of Carson Sawyer I just thought that part of my past had ended."

Billy turned and stumbled out of the trading post. He sat on the bench on the front porch of the trading post contemplating a plan. He finally arrived at the point where he knew he was enjoying life like never before. He had thoughts of finding a girl, settling down, and raising a bunch of children. Billy laughed at the thought of a bunch of little Billys running around.

Stony McGraw and Johnnie Butler found Billy thinking and laughing. Stony stepped up on the porch.

"I don't know who you are talking to, but they must have told a funny one."

"No, I was just thinking about having a bunch of kids like me running around the house. That would be some kind of hoot, don't you think?"

Stony stared at Billy for a moment. He never heard him talk about the matter of getting himself hitched and having children.

"This place is getting to you, Billy. I swear it sounds like all you need is a pretty girl to walk by and you will be done for."

Something caught the attention of Johnnie and he

turned to see a woman riding a horse coming toward the trading post.

"Boys, we have trouble riding in. That is one of the girls from the wagon train. Billy, I think she fell sweet on you, too."

Rachael reined up at the hitching post in front of the trading post.

"To what do we owe this glorious pleasure I might ask?"

Billy stood and held his hat over his heart.

"I don't want to ride on that wagon any longer, and my back hurts from riding this horse. I want to stay right here and I thought I could talk one of you gentlemen into taking me in. I am ready to settle."

While she talked, Rachael's eyes never left Billy.

"We don't have much in the way of accommodations for a lady like you, Rachael. I would like for you to stay, but I don't know where I could put you. Why don't you unfork that horse and you and I can put our heads together to see what we can come up with."

Stony turned to Johnnie.

"It has been a long time since I have heard wedding bells, but I think I hear them going off right now."

"That is a bell on that cow yonder, Stony. But I do think you are right."

Billy escorted Rachael to the Flapjack Café. He held out his arm for her and she took it. Stony and Johnnie trailed behind.

15

Four days after his death, the body of Chief Ehane came down from high above the ground and a sacred burial took place near a massive oak tree. Red Feather called for a council. He wanted Boots and Migisi to attend.

"My father has given me the four arrows of sweet medicine. They stand for many laws. We have two for hunting and two for war."

Red Feather held up the four arrows tied together in a bundle. This showed the other elders that Chief Ehane picked his successor and passed the arrows to Red Feather.

"This is what my father taught me and it is what I will continue as his son and as your chief. First, I will be a peacemaker. If my son is killed in front of my teepee, I will take the peace pipe and smoke. Then I will be called an honest chief. Second, I will protect our land and our people. If our braves should become scared and retreat, I will not take a step back, but I will take a stand to protect you and your land. Third, I will get out and talk to people. Fourth, If strangers come, I will give them gifts and invitations. Next, if anyone comes to my teepee asking for something, I will never refuse. I will step outside and sing my chief song so that all the people will know I have done something good. These are some of the teachings I have learned from my father Chief Ehane. Be with me, my mother, and my sister so that we will not become lonely. If my mother wishes to stay in her teepee, that is where she will stay. I know there are those among you who wish to be chief. It is my duty, and if I should fall, the duty will go to my sister Migisi."

Red Feather paused to let the words sink in. His last statement caused much murmuring among the elders. A woman had never been chief before and some thought it would be wrong. However, Migisi's stature in the village was stronger than the elders.

"My sister is made for chief. My father said it would be so and he is here with us in this council. Migisi could out ride, out run, and out fight any brave in her group. I saw her do those things. It would be an honor for this village to have the first woman chief, and If something happens to me, it will be so."

Migisi sat with a blank expression on her face. Inwardly she felt as though she had been caught off guard by Red

Feather's remarks, especially those about her father. She and her father had a close bond, but she never guessed he would want her to be chief. Her father was always forward thinking, and it would mark a historical event for her to wear the chief's bonnet. If it came to be that she assumed the role of Chief, Migisi would accept the honor. She smiled at the thought.

"When we finish our council, there will be a celebration for Chief Ehane and the Great Spirit. There I will sing the chief's son as my father taught me."

The eleven elders each took a puff from the pipe and passed it to the next. That act signified acceptance of Chief Red Feather and his words. After the elders finished, Red Feather rose to meet each one as they left his lodge. They openly showed their support.

Migisi tried to check her tears as she embraced her brother.

Migisi spent a couple of days talking with the elders. They told her the women in the village wanted her to be chief and if the women wanted that, then that should happen. Migisi grew up with many of the younger women and the older women have understood for many years that Chief Ehane wanted her to take his place when he leaves.

Migisi knew it would be hard to act as chief with a mountain man husband and she would be away from her children and grandchildren.

"My husband, we must take our family to our cave. The grandchildren have never seen our home, and we need to sit and talk these latest things over. I am ready to leave when you are ready to leave."

"My wife wants to go to her home. She has talked with her mother and Nokomis said she should take her family and go home for a while. I want to make sure you, Red Feather, know I will do as your sister pleases. If you want her here, please send for her. We will stay a while, and then stop here on the way to our trading post."

"You have done well for my sister. Go to your home, and take peace with you."

Red Feather embraced Boots and afterward turned to enter the chief's lodge.

Packing for two people is one thing, but packing for two people plus four is something else. Fortunately, pack burros were able to handle the loads and after a day of work, everyone started for the wide track to go up the mountain to the cave Boots and Migisi called home. Blue Sky and Little Feather were sad to leave their new friends, but they were also excited to see where their grandparents lived.

"This place is unbelievable. This is as close to heaven as you can get without actually being there."

Little Feather stood on the huge rock porch that jutted out from the cave. She saw the park to the right, a few more steps and she found the corral where Boots and Little Boots were putting the horses and burros. The mountainside lay in front of her with a thick forest of firs, pines, and spruce.

Boots put his arm on the shoulders of his grand-daughter.

"From where you are standing, we have seen wolves, elk, moose, deer, big horn sheep, black bears, grizzly bears, coyotes, and mountain lions. Soon, your father and I will hunt a killer mountain lion. It comes too close to our corral and we tried to move it to a new territory. I believe the big cat is back. I saw tracks on our way up here."

"Will it be dangerous?"

"We know how to hunt the mountain lion. There is always some danger in anything you attempt on this mountain, but wisdom helps remove most of it."

"Is Blue going on the hunt?"

"I am going to ask him to stay here and with my rifle keep a close watch in case the big cat comes back around. We must always protect ourselves."

Little Feather had the same expression when she finally went into the cave. She could not believe the size of the cave, and the stream running at the very back had the coldest water. She saw buffalo robes hanging from the ceiling of the cave to provide separate rooms. A fire pit sat on the porch, and another cooking fire pit sat inside the cave.

"Mother, why do we have two fire pits?"

Ayashe told her daughter the fire pit on the porch stayed lit during the good weather. When cold weather, snow, and blizzards hit during winter, the inside fire pit was put to use.

Migisi appeared wearing her buckskin pants and shirt. She motioned for Little Feather to come to sit by her near the outside fire pit. A small blaze started when they first arrived home.

"I want to tell you about our people, why we are here, and I would like to teach you medicine. It will take a long time, but we have plenty of that."

Migisi told Little Feather how she and Boots met during rendezvous and how they planned to run away together. They did run away, but they were found by Red Feather who did not want Migisi to be with Boots. Chief Ehane eventually stepped in and blessed the union. The stories continued into the night. Nobody noticed Boots and Little Boots were gone. Blue sat on the porch with his grandfather's rifle in his lap. He loved being on the Rocky Mountains and he felt completely grown up around his grandfather. Blue took his duty to protect if the mountain lion returned seriously and he kept scanning with his eyes.

16

Mountain man Boots hunted with his son Little Boots for many years. They knew the moves of one another so well one could be exact in knowing where the other hunter went. They quickly separated and went in different directions. Little Boots headed for the park where he and his father camped years ago. Boots searched for the tracks he picked up on his way to the cave. When he found the tracks, he followed the trail. Both hunters walked with a light step. Squirrels scampered across the forest floor, birds continued their songs, and Boots felt comfortable knowing the animals were not aware of his presence in the forest. He knew he followed the trail of the big killer cat. Once, he stopped. He could smell the cat for a moment, but the scent disappeared. The breeze was in his favor and he knew he came close to the mountain lion. He continued on the trail, keeping the breeze in his face. He also detected the scent of rain, and Boots hoped the rain would stall long enough for him to find the lion. He stopped again.

Boots slowly turned his head to his right. He felt the presence of something watching him on his right side. Clouds darkened the sky for a moment and the sun barely broke through the trees. He spotted a black wolf looking at him. The wolf sat on his rear haunches and showed no signs of attack. Suddenly a rushing sound shattered the quiet and the wolf stood and trotted away. Boots needed to find the source of the new noise. The noise caused the birds to quit chattering. The squirrels disappeared, and Boots knew something disturbed the environment.

After a brief pause, Boots continued walking. The trail took him down toward a valley where there were several switchbacks working to the bottom of the valley. He carefully placed one foot in front of the other. It would take hours to reach the bottom at this rate, but Boots knew to be careful and alert. The terrain favored a mountain lion. They liked to be above their prey and the powerful cat would leap to land on the back. Boots knew if that happened on the narrow path he would be in trouble. Boots knew there would be another way to the bottom of the canyon. He slowly and carefully turned to try to get back to the starting point on the switch back. That is when he looked into the yellow eyes of the biggest mountain lion he had ever seen.

The big cat sat low to the ground, ready to pounce. The cat knew it would not be a good opportunity to pounce because the jump would have to be perfect or he would miss and tumble down the side of the canyon.

Boots heard the vicious growl come from the lungs of the mountain lion. He knew that if the cat pounced, he could duck under and the cat would miss and wind up dead. That would not be a bad option, Boots thought, because the mountain lion had him dead to rights.

A rustling of the leaves did not distract the lion's focus. When Boots moved, the cat would track the movement with his head. Boots heard a whoosh of air and he saw an arrow stab into the side of the mountain lion. That caused the cat to rise and run. Boots got a good look at the huge animal and he realized he was moments away from death.

Little Boots peeked from around the trunk of a spruce tree.

"Are you alright down there?"

The best voice Boots had ever heard asked that question.

"I am fine and dandy, but you missed the kill. The arrow hit the side instead of the head."

Boots scrambled to the tree where Little Boots hid.

"I know I missed, but I didn't trust the arrow enough to aim at the head. The shaft felt a little old and flimsy, so I took the best shot I could."

"I am glad you did because you saved me from certain death."

Boots breathed a little easier. He knew he could have outwitted the mountain lion, but his son made a crucial decision to aim at the cat. Boots would always appreciate the actions of his son, and the story would be that he saved his father's life.

"I don't know so much about saving your life, Father. That cat was nervous about jumping you and I think if he did, you could have pushed him off in the air. I did get him away from the edge of that cliff though."

"He won't be hard to trail. We can follow the blood dots and put an end to that killer."

Boots told him about the lion deciding that attacking humans was not all that bad. Unless they were hungry, mountain lions normally shied away from men. This one, however, seemed to like the easy prey.

Boots and Little Boots separated by about a hundred yards. Little Boots stayed on the blood trail while Boots surveyed the forest ahead.

Boots heard a bird call and stopped. It was the call of a bird that did not make its home in the Rocky Mountains. He turned to his left and saw Little Boots frozen in place looking straight ahead.

He had found the mountain lion. The big cat lay on its side. The arrow from Little Boots' bow stuck in the lion's side. Little Boots watched the arrow move with every breath the lion took.

Boots saw the mountain lion and started to move

around to the backside. He stepped quietly, but he knew that was not necessary. The lion had taken its last step.

When he was about ten feet upwind behind the huge cat, Boots jumped and seemingly flew through the air and landed with both hands on the throat of the mountain lion. The cat was much bigger than Boots anticipated, and he thought it would be a tough struggle to squeeze the life of out him, but his hands closed on the throat.

After several intense moments, Boots felt the mountain lion lose the battle and he did not take another breath. Boots stood and worked the cramps out of his hands.

Little Boots pulled his arrow from the cat.

"You took him out, Father. I would have never thought a fellow could do what you just did."

The old mountain man squatted near the carcass of the mountain lion as he looked up to his son. This was a moment for both of them to remember.

"The mountain has been good to me."

That was all that Boots could muster at the moment.

Little Boots found a long limb and they tied the front and rear paws of the mountain lion to the limb. They each lifted an end of the limb and with Boots leading the way in front, headed for the cave.

"Your mother will show her grandchildren how to make a pelt. We will not eat this lion. There is a place near the cave where we can put the carcass to feed other animals. He will return to the mountain that way."

The Rocky Mountain killer was no longer on the loose.

Mountain Man Boots sees the little community around the trading post grow even more. A new doctor helps and his daughter marries with a newborn soon on the way. A trick shooter Rootin' Tootin' Shootin' Billy Pine has turned into an entertainer extraordinaire and continues to delight wagon train travelers with his skills. He marries, and another newborn is soon on the way. Will Migisi become the first woman Cheyenne Chief? That question will be answered!

Made in United States
North Haven, CT
09 October 2023

42556758R00074